"NO ONE DOES
MALE FRIENDSHIP
(OR VOMIT AND
ACCIDENTAL NUDITY)
BETTER THAN
ANDREW SMITH."
—S. A. Bodeen,
author of *The Compound*

"I'M NOT SURE I'VE EVER
LAUGHED MORE WITH,
CRIED MORE WITH,
AND ROOTED HARDER
FOR A CHARACTER THAN
FINN EASTON.
HIS VOICE IS SO STRONG,
SO REAL, THAT HIS TRIUMPHS
AND FAILURES FELT LIKE
THEY WERE MY OWN.
I SERIOUSLY LOVED THIS BOOK."
—Len Vlahos,
author of *The Scar Boys*

100 SIDEWAYS MILES

Also by Andrew Smith

Winger

Stand-Off

100 SIDEWAYS MILES

ANDREW SMITH

SIMON & SCHUSTER BFYR

New York London Toronto Sydney New Delhi

For my mother and father, whose atoms are scattering

SIMON & SCHUSTER BFYR

An imprint of Simon & Schuster Children's Publishing Division
1230 Avenue of the Americas, New York, New York 10020

SIMON & SCHUSTER BFYR is a trademark of Simon & Schuster, Inc.
For information about special discounts for bulk purchases, please contact Simon & Schuster
Special Sales at 1-866-506-1949 or business@simonandschuster.com.
The Simon & Schuster Speakers Bureau can bring authors to your live event.
For more information or to book an event, contact the Simon & Schuster Speakers Bureau
at 1-866-248-3049 or visit our website at www.simonspeakers.com.
Also available in a SIMON & SCHUSTER BFYR hardcover edition
Book design and photo-illustration by Lucy Ruth Cummins
The text for this book is set in Adobe Caslon Pro.
Manufactured in the United States of America
First SIMON & SCHUSTER BFYR paperback edition September 2015
2 4 6 8 10 9 7 5 3 1
The Library of Congress has cataloged the hardcover edition as follows:
Smith, Andrew (Andrew Anselmo), 1959–
100 sideways miles / Andrew Smith.
pages cm
Summary: Finn Easton, sixteen and epileptic, struggles to feel like more than just a
character in his father's cult-classic novels with the help of his best friend,
Cade Hernandez, and first love, Julia, until Julia moves away.
ISBN 978-1-4424-4495-9 (hardcover) — ISBN 978-1-4424-4497-3 (eBook)
[1. Best friends—Fiction. 2. Friendship—Fiction. 3. Fathers and sons—Fiction. 4. Authors—
Fiction. 5. Dating (Social customs)—Fiction. 6. Epilepsy—Fiction. 7. California—Fiction.]
I. Title. II. Title: One hundred sideways miles.
PZ7.S64257Aag 2014
[Fic]—dc23
2013030326
ISBN 978-1-4424-4496-6 (paperback)

ACKNOWLEDGMENTS

I dedicated this book to my mother and father, whose disapproval of my teenage announcement that I wanted to become a writer motivated me—a true teenager, after all—to do exactly that.

Sometimes I stare out across the sky at night and, like a lot of people, I wonder where we really are and what else is out there, and especially about how fast we are going. I think I caught that wonder from my teachers—the special ones—all the way through the miles and miles between kindergarten and graduate school.

I also had much inspiration from Bowie, my daughter's heterochromatic dog, whom I would never send into space.

Also, this book would never have been written if it weren't for the following: Sleeplessness, Self-Doubt, Depression, and Anxiety. So, thank you, demons. You guys are the greatest! I don't know what I would do without you!

And finally, again, to the beehive that is Simon & Schuster: Thank you to David Gale, my editor; Justin Chanda, my publisher and a man with remarkable taste in music; Navah Wolfe, associate editor; Paul Crichton and Siena Koncsol in publicity; all the wonderful education and library people; copyeditor Lara Stelmaszyk; and Lucy Ruth Cummins, who makes books look so beautiful.

AUTHOR'S NOTE

There are only a few things in this book that are actually true. Most of the places are contrivances of fiction. The most notable exception is San Francisquito Canyon, which is located in northern Los Angeles County. The canyon is very much as described in this book, and the ruins of William Mulholland's great failure still lie scattered in the creekbed at the bottom. There is no museum on the site, however, but there probably should be. As for the other places: Burnt Mill Creek and Aberdeen Lake do not exist anywhere outside the pages of this story.

PART 1

THE PERIGEE MOON

THE QUIT MISSION

Look: I do not know where I actually came from. I wonder, I suspect, but I do not know.

I am not the only one who sometimes thinks I came from the pages of a book my father wrote. Maybe it's like that for all boys of a certain—or uncertain—age: We feel as though there are no choices we'd made through all those miles and miles behind us that hadn't been scripted by our fathers, and that our futures are only a matter of flipping the next page that was written ahead of us.

I am not the only one who's ever been trapped inside a book.

A story involving alien visitors from outer space, an epileptic kid who doesn't really know where he came from, knackeries and dead horses falling a hundred sideways miles, abandoned prisons, a shadow play, moons and stars, and jumping from a bridge into a flood should probably begin with a big explosion in the sky about fourteen billion years ago. After all, the whole story is rather biblical, isn't it?

Poof!

But it doesn't.

It begins at a high school in Burnt Mill Creek, California. It begins before the summer Cade Hernandez and I went on a fact-finding expedition to visit a college in Oklahoma.

We didn't quite make it to the college. I'm not sure if we found any facts, either.

Mr. Nossik hung motivational posters on the walls of his classroom—things about perseverance, integrity, and shit like that.

One of them said this:

OPPORTUNITY: WHEN ONE DOOR CLOSES,
ANOTHER ONE OPENS.

The first time we saw that one, Cade Hernandez, my best friend, said, "Sounds like he lives in a fucking haunted house."

I suppose it was a year for opening doors in more ways than I ever imagined.

At Burnt Mill Creek High School, the people in charge were constantly on some kind of pointless mission to get us kids to quit doing shit. All schools everywhere are like that, I think. Quit Chewing Gum flopped in ninth grade. Quit Using Cell Phones was dead before it started. And, now, during the second semester of our junior year, the quit mission involved "fuck."

Not doing it, saying it.

It was destined to fail.

More than a century of public education that aimed its pedagogical crosshairs at getting teenagers to quit having sex, quit drinking, quit driving so fast, quit taking drugs, never had the slightest behavior-altering effect on kids.

Not that I did any of those things. Well, some of them.

Now we were caught up in the Burnt Mill Creek High School mission to make us quit saying "fuck," which is more or less a comma—a punctuation mark—to most teenagers when they speak.

The teachers and administrators at Burnt Mill Creek High School might just as well have focused their energies on getting tectonic plates to quit making so many fucking earthquakes.

The brains behind the Quit Saying "Fuck" mission was our history teacher, Mr. Nossik. He and the staff at the school painted signs with slogans that said things like NO F-BOMBS, PLEASE! (the kids called them "fuck posters"), and teachers even wore specially printed WATCH YOUR LANGUAGE, O PIONEERS! T-shirts. The kids called them "fuck shirts."

The campaign only made things worse.

By May, Mr. Nossik was about to explode.

We were all about to witness a Nazi having a stroke.

Here is what happened: Our teacher, Mr. Nossik, believed in making history "come alive." So, naturally, on May 7, which was the anniversary of the German surrender in World War II, Mr. Nossik dressed himself up as a Gestapo *kommissar.*

Naturally.

What a nice scene: a Nazi at the front of a public-school classroom filled with sixteen-year-old boys and girls.

You can't make history come alive. History is deader than Laika the space dog.

And I'll admit it—nobody in my class ever learned anything from Mr. Nossik's living displays. Are you kidding me? This was eleventh grade. Shit like that stopped working on our brains around the same time the training wheels came off our bicycles.

Besides, Mr. Nossik's so-called "living history" often pushed things a little too far. One time last March, he dressed up as a battered drowning victim to commemorate the catastrophic failure of the St. Francis Dam.

History lives, it dies, and it comes alive again as the soaking-wet, mangled, and bloodied corpse of a Mexican ranch hand.

My mother was a Jew, which technically makes me a Jew. Only a few people know that about me because on the surface I am an atheist; and with a name like Finn Easton, who would guess I'd feel a bit edgy around a forty-five-year-old freak who liked to role-play genocidal war criminals?

I am named after the Mark Twain character, by the way.

I am *not* named after the Finn in my father's book; I swear.

So: My best friend, Cade Hernandez, who always sat next to me unless Mr. Nossik kicked him out of class or assigned him a back-row desk facing away from the lectern (just because Mr. Nossik frequently couldn't stand looking at Cade), raised his hand and asked our Nazi leader this: "Mr. Nossik, why do I always get a boner in this class, at exactly eight-fifteen, every morning? This is ridiculous!"

Kids laughed.

I laughed.

Who *wouldn't* laugh at a boy who asked a Nazi a question about getting an erection?

Besides, Cade Hernandez was our de facto commander in

the Stop Trying to Make Us Stop revolution, our act of defiance against the quit missions. Cade Hernandez ran the school. He could get anyone to do anything he wanted. Cade Hernandez was magic or something.

Mr. Nossik's face reddened, which, in the aesthetic arrangement of things, matched the color scheme of his outfit perfectly.

Let me tell you something else about Cade Hernandez: As the school's de facto commander in the Stop Trying to Make Us Stop revolution, he was an expert button pusher. The moment any authority figure challenged Cade's control over things, the game was on.

Mr. Nossik despised Cade Hernandez as deeply as anyone could ever hate another person.

It was only a matter of time until Mr. Nossik came up with some type of Quit Being Cade Hernandez mission.

To be honest, all us kids in the class loved to see the two of them square off. Cade routinely won. At least once a week, Mr. Nossik would tell Cade that he couldn't stand looking at him anymore, so he'd order Cade to the back of the room, as far away from Mr. Nossik's desk as possible.

And Cade frequently wasn't doing anything to justify his banishment.

But Cade Hernandez did have a way of just staring and staring—without blinking—calmly showing the faintest trace of a smile on his face as though he were saying, *Come on, fucker, let's see who wins today.*

That was it.

Cade stared and stared and smiled and smiled.

And that was how he looked at Mr. Nossik on May 7, Nazi

Day, when Cade Hernandez, in as straightforward and sincere a voice as you could ever imagine, asked our Gestapo *kommissar* teacher why he got a boner during history class at the same time every morning.

This was Cade Hernandez, a kid whose lower-body blood flow apparently had tidal predictability.

Mr. Nossik, his voice quavering as though he'd just swallowed a fistful of feathers and sand, stamped his jackbooted foot and told Cade to GET OUT of the classroom immediately.

Man! The only thing that could possibly have made Mr. Nossik look *more* like Hitler at that moment would have been a toothbrush swath of black hair on his upper lip.

And Cade, all innocence and self-pity, said, "Can I wait a couple minutes before I stand up, please, Mr. Nossik? Seriously, this thing is ridiculous!"

We all laughed again.

And Mr. Nossik—in a voice reminiscent of the most fiery Nuremberg Rally oratory—stamped and shrieked, "GET! OUT!"

So Cade Hernandez, smiling slightly, completely unashamed, stood and walked across the room to wait outside the door while the quaking Mr. Nossik composed himself.

Of course, everyone looked to see if Cade really *did* have a boner.

I'm not saying.

And Mr. Nossik, our Gestapo *kommissar*, didn't actually have a stroke that morning, but I believe some crucial arteries and shit inside vital parts of his body got dangerously close to their bursting point every time Cade Hernandez put pressure on Mr. Nossik's hair-trigger nerves.

ANDREW SMITH

Cade Hernandez and I both played baseball for the Burnt Mill Creek High School Pioneers baseball team.

O Pioneers!

Cade was our pitcher—a lefty who'd been scouted by the majors, extremely talented—and I played the outfield, usually right. I would not want to play a position like pitcher, where there is such a high likelihood of making costly mistakes.

Costly mistakes, like sexual confusion and nuclear weapons, which by the way are both legacies passed down from the greatest generation—the guys who whipped Hitler—are strongly related to extinction.

Who wants that?

Cade's nickname was Win-Win, but it had nothing to do with his record as a starter. I will explain later, since I wanted this part of the story to be about me: Finn Easton.

TWENTY MILES PER SECOND

Here is what I believe: Distance is more important than time.

The earth travels about twenty miles every second.

It's easy enough to figure out: π, our distance from the sun, three hundred sixty-five days, and there you go.

Twenty miles per second.

In the same amount of time it takes Cade Hernandez to drive us from my house in San Francisquito Canyon to the town of Burnt Mill Creek and our school, Planet Earth carries us about eighteen thousand miles from the exact spot where we were when we started out. It's equivalent to driving three-fourths of the way around the world at the equator.

Think about it: That's quite a commute to get to school just to see some withered old man dressed up as Charles Lindbergh or Betsy Ross.

Oh, yeah: Mr. Nossik was never afraid of cross-dressing.

Cade picks me up every day because I am not allowed to drive. I have seizures and blank out sometimes. I call it "blanking out" because things don't get "black," like some people might say. When a seizure comes on, to be honest, everything looks especially beautiful.

I don't have them too often, and I am told there is a good chance that I will grow out of the condition.

I believe I will miss it.

My seizures always begin the same way: I smell flowers. Then all the words empty out of my head, and everything is just there: a chaotic jumble of patternless, nameless clusters of atoms.

Beautiful.

My condition is a souvenir from the day a dead horse fell out of the sky and landed on me and my mother.

I was born on the anniversary of the first-ever atom bomb explosion on Planet Earth.

A gift from the greatest generation—the guys who saved the world!

July 16.

Some of those atoms—when set free in 1945 into the atmosphere above the New Mexico desert—found their way into me: my hands, my head, and my heart.

My atoms have been on this Finn trip for almost eleven billion miles.

Just about every individual atom in the universe, every last bit of the stuff that builds me, is nearly fourteen billion years old. Think of that distance: fourteen billion times all those hundreds of millions of miles.

I hold together pretty well, considering how much my atoms have been through.

These are things I think about sometimes.

Look: I realize now that I wasn't only trapped inside my father's book; my father also did not want to let go of me. Maybe that's an egotistical thing to say—we are all centers of our personal universes in any event—but it was ironically obvious to me; and my father had told me straight out, anyway.

He said to me, "Finn, I wish you would never grow up and go away."

So that summer of the Perseids and the perigee moon, of Julia Bishop and the abandoned prison at Aberdeen Lake, of finding myself stranded so far away from home along with my best friend, really turned out to be a sort of scripted shadow play in which the epileptic boy could choose for himself whether or not he would ever get out of the book.

What was I going to do?

I am an epileptic. I blank out.

I also have heterochromatic eyes, which means they are different colors. Green and blue, if you need to know. People almost never notice it, because most people are afraid to look at other peoples' eyes. I know that because when you have heterochromatic eyes, you *always* look at eyes—always trying to find someone else who is like you, like we come from a different planet or something.

Cade Hernandez noticed it one day when we sat in my backyard hot tub together, the summer before eighth grade. Cade Hernandez wasn't afraid of anything, especially not looking directly at another guy's eyes.

I have never found another heterochromatic set of eyes to

look at, except for ones on the Internet. And they were probably Photoshopped, anyway.

You know what they say about your imagination being limitless? Well, that is absolute horseshit. You can't imagine anything if you don't already have a word for it in your head.

Trust me, I know.

If you really want to imagine something, try imagining what it would be like to empty every word from your head and then look at the universe. You'll see nothing at all that you could ever understand. There will be no separation or distinction between object, color, temperature, or sound; there will be neither borders nor edges, no limits or size, and you will smell things and not have any idea at all what is happening.

I get that way sometimes. My head empties out, and I smell something like nameless flowers.

I have never been outside the state of California in the nearly seventeen years that my atoms and molecules have been stuck together, walking around and calling themselves Finn.

Oklahoma, where Cade and I were planning to visit over our last summer vacation from Burnt Mill Creek High School, might just as well have been in a different galaxy as far as my atoms were concerned.

There is actually more empty space between our atoms and molecules than anything solid. It's as though we're all clouds of gas, optical illusions—like how spokes on a spinning bicycle wheel blur invisibly into a solid barrier between *hereandthere*, *thisside* and *thatside*.

It's a wonder we don't all just float away—*pfft!*—like smoke.

At first, Dad tried to explain it to me as this: My mother simply floated away when I was seven years old.

In truth, a dead horse fell on us.

I know that is an absurd thing to consider—a dead horse falling out of the sky—but it actually happened.

Picture this: We lived in a small cabin in the Sierras of northern California, at a place called Wheelerville, which is located on the Salmon Creek.

Wheelerville was named for Wheeler Caverns, a cave formation. Near the entrance to the caves, there is a bridge across the Salmon Creek Gorge, popular among base parachutists and other crazy people who like to jump from the edge of the span with enormous wrappings of elastic lashed to their ankles. The bridge is aptly named the Salmon Creek Gorge Bridge.

Although I don't remember it, the story went like this: My mother and I were walking along the creek beneath the bridge when a truck from a knackery, which is what some people call a rendering plant, overturned on the span above us.

Look: A dead horse fell from the bridge. Nobody thought to lash bungee cords to the animal's legs, or maybe equip it with a parachute.

That would have been something to see.

Things like that turn men into writers and other, worse things.

I don't remember it.

After all, it happened more than five billion miles ago.

The knackery truck was on its way to the plant after picking up a twenty-two-year-old Percheron gelding. The horse was dead, set to be rendered, to have its atoms turned into pet food and stuff like shampoos, lubricants on condoms, rubber tires, and explosives.

Did you know they put dead animals into bombs?

My father told me once, *If that doesn't make you a poet, Finn, nothing will.*

I would rather be a poet than end up inside a bomb or a bottle of shampoo.

There is something important in running a knackery.

When you think about it, the universe is nothing but this vast knackery of churning black holes and exploding stars, constantly freeing atoms that collect together and become something else, and something else again.

Here is what I think about that horse falling on us: I figure it took a little more than four seconds for the horse to travel from the span of the bridge, over three hundred feet above, to where my mother and I stood on the bank of Salmon Creek. During that fall, the earth moved approximately one hundred miles. If you were to walk a straight line for a hundred miles and drop a total of three hundred feet, you wouldn't even realize you were descending in elevation at all.

That horse fell one hundred sideways miles.

Look: There are scars along my back where they put pins in me to heal the vertebrae.

They look like colon, vertical slash, colon. Like this:

:|:

I am fine now.

In baseball, I have a good arm and a bat, and I can field, but I am not interested in playing it after high school. My natural talent, I think, is in being *fine*—no matter what is actually going on inside me.

I am fine.

Nobody ever thinks otherwise.

:|:

FIVE EUROS IN DOLLARS

There is no creek in Burnt Mill Creek. I don't know if there was a creek here at one time, or if the people who named our town were attempting to fool settlers into populating this barren valley at the bottom of San Francisquito Canyon.

False advertising.

There's no mill here either.

Maybe it burned.

Atoms will be freed, after all, and names are misleading and can constantly change. And people hide themselves in costumes.

That's what I believe, at least, and so far it has pretty much been the story of my life.

Cade Hernandez was like a god.

When we were in tenth grade, he orchestrated a plan to standardize our entire class—make every tenth-grader exactly the same. He called it our Quit Being Individuals mission. With only about two hundred kids in our class, it wasn't a difficult task to manage, and like I said, Cade Hernandez had the ability to make anyone do whatever he wanted.

After all, Cade explained, it was exactly what the school system had been trying to do to us for our entire lives: make us all the same. So at the end of our sophomore year as the week for the State of California Basic Educational Standards Test (they called it the BEST Test) neared and hundreds of number two pencils were being sharpened in preparation for hours of mindless bubble filling by the kids at Burnt Mill Creek High School, Cade Hernandez came up with a wicked idea; one that he got every tenth-grader in our school to play along with too.

Cade's plan was simple. Even the dumbest kids could follow it.

The plan involved having every one of us give exactly the same pattern of responses on the BEST Test. And we all did it too. When the testing week came around, every single sophomore at Burnt Mill Creek High School bubbled in the following four responses, over and over and over:

C-A-D-E

Naturally, I'd expressed my skepticism over the lack of *B*s, but Cade argued that it didn't matter, since the only people who gave a shit about the BEST Test were bureaucrats and politicians.

"Well, what if they close our school down and fire all the teachers or something?" I'd said.

"Really, Finn? *Really?*"

Cade Hernandez could even get *me* to do whatever he wanted.

And we did not find out until the following year just how effective Cade Hernandez's Quit Being Individuals mission would actually turn out to be.

· · ·

Like most of the boys who played ball for the Burnt Mill Creek High School Pioneers, Cade "Win-Win" Hernandez chewed tobacco.

I did not, however.

I think the boys on the team never would have picked up the habit if our coaches didn't do it so often; if they never spoke the praises of the tradition of chewing tobacco in the dugout, like it was part of becoming a man, part of the game itself.

Our batting coach, a man named John Ritchey, had such rotten gums from his habit of tobacco chewing that he actually lost one of his lower incisors during a practice session. He didn't care at all. Coach Ritchey spit the entire tooth—root and all—onto the clay of the batting cage at Pioneer Field. The tooth looked like one of those Halloween candy corns that had been boiled in sewage. Most of the boys watched in a kind of hero worship combined with fear and tobacco-buzzed disgust.

Coach Ritchey's tooth became a sort of religious artifact for the team, like the bones or dried innards from a Catholic saint. Somebody—and I am certain it was Cade Hernandez—must have picked the thing up, because Coach Ritchey's rotten tooth had a way of showing up in a randomly selected boy's sanitaries, cap, or athletic supporter before every game we played.

It was such good fun.

"One of these days, they are going to kick you out of school for all the shit you do, and I will have to walk here, or hitchhike and risk getting picked up by a child molester or some shit," I said.

"Your dad or stepmom would drive you," Cade said.

"I don't want to ride with my parents. What eleventh-grade boy rides with his parents? They treat me like too much of a baby as it is. I'd rather take my chances with the molesters."

Cade Hernandez drove a two-year-old Toyota pickup. Every day, we left school for lunch but came back for last-period baseball practice. Our season ended that first week in May, not so victoriously for the Burnt Mill Creek High School Pioneers.

We'll get 'em next year.

Cade looked me over and answered, "I think you're safe as far as perverts are concerned, Finn. Just sayin'. I mean, you're pretty damn ugly."

"Yeah."

Of course he was joking. Cade Hernandez and I looked so much alike that people who didn't know us often thought we were brothers. We both were tall and bony, and blond headed, too. Cade kept his hair trimmed short, and he had a very sparse golden beard that went from his sideburns and curled almost invisibly just around the lower edge of his jaw. I didn't have the first nub growing out of my face yet, and my hair was long and unruly.

Cade Hernandez's parents were immigrants from Argentina. He made up wild stories about being the great-grandson of an escaped Nazi-breeding-camp doctor.

I think the stories were probably true, given the color of Cade's hair, his blue eyes, and the paleness of his skin. It probably was also a compelling reason behind Cade's messing with Mr. Nossik in class that morning of the Nazi display.

Cade Hernandez and I had been friends since I was ten years old. That's a lot of miles traveled together—about six billion.

We met in elementary school. Cade Hernandez was my first real friend. His family lived in Burnt Mill Creek, and when I enrolled in grade five, my family, which consisted at that time of my father and pregnant stepmother, had just moved to San Francisquito Canyon.

It wasn't until the summer before eighth grade that I told Cade Hernandez about the dead horse in the sky. I believe he naturally assumed Tracy, my stepmother, was my actual mother. After all, I called her Mom.

That was the day Cade leaned over toward me, so close our shoulders touched, and he said, "Holy shit, Finn. Your eyes are different colors."

I said, "They call that heterochromatism."

"Fucking cool."

At that time I also said to him, "Not only that, but I am a Jew."

I remember the day perfectly. We sat in the hot tub beside my backyard swimming pool. It was summer vacation. I had had a particularly bad seizure the day before. I'd pissed myself. Cade didn't know about it, but sometimes, afterward, I felt like I wanted to die. Sitting there in just a bathing suit, not really thinking about anything, Cade became curious about the emoticon scar along my spine. So I told him my back had been broken when a dead horse fell out of the sky and killed my mother.

I told him about knackeries, and about being a Jew.

Cade answered, "What the hell does *that* mean?"

"Well," I said, "my real mother was a Jew. That makes me a Jew."

"What goes along with being a Jew?" Cade asked me. "Secret handshakes?"

I shrugged. "I don't know. I'm not a real Jew or anything. I don't even believe in God to begin with."

"You're going to all kinds of hell, Finn," Cade said.

"No. I'm pretty sure my atoms will just be scattered out there like everyone else's."

"That's scary," Cade said.

"Well, I just wanted to tell you, in case you decide to hate me for being a Jew," I said.

I had been wondering about this ever since Cade told me the stories about his Nazi-breeding-camp great-grandfather.

"You're fucking dumb," Cade said.

That was how eighth-grade boys told each other everything was *okay*.

:|:

And then Cade Hernandez said, "The tracks left in the snow by a horse with a ridiculously big hard-on."

I said, "What?"

"That's what that shit on your back looks like, Finn. If a horse with a really big boner left tracks in snow, 'cause you're so fucking white. It's fucking awesome."

:|:

So, on Mr. Nossik's Nazi Day, we had lunch at Flat Face Pizza. Cade and I ate there at least twice a week because the food was free for us.

Cade Hernandez worked in the kitchen and delivered pizza for Flat Face Pizza. The sign above the business, which was one of the dozen or so boxes of storefronts along Old Mill Boulevard, was an enormous, perfectly round pizza with a grinning face painted on it.

Clever.

It looked like it had been done by a six-year-old.

Cade Hernandez's nickname was Win-Win.

He got that nickname at the start of our junior year at Burnt Mill Creek. A senior girl, an exchange student from Germany named Monica Fassbinder, had a peculiar attraction to Cade Hernandez. Monica Fassbinder would pay Cade five dollars every time he'd allow her to give him a hand job at school, in the shed where the night custodian parked his electric golf cart.

Cade Hernandez used the money he earned to buy cans of chewing tobacco, and we joked that Monica Fassbinder's obsession with giving Cade hand jobs was a win-win proposition as long as they never got caught.

They never did get caught, and that was where the nickname came from.

Cade was always in a good mood.

Cade Hernandez always had plenty of tobacco, too. Win-Win Hernandez earned a steady income of about thirty dollars a week from Monica's hand jobs.

Monica Fassbinder caused Cade Hernandez to free a lot of his atoms in the night-custodian's shed.

My father bristles around Cade, avoids him as much as possible. But I think Cade has magical spell-casting beams or something that he can fire from his eyes, because I'd never seen a girl—my stepmother and sister included—who didn't think Cade Hernandez was endlessly adorable, even if he did things such as openly announce the frequency and stubbornness of his erections.

Some guys have all the luck.

Win. Win.

When we finished our pizza, Cade asked me, "How much is five euros in dollars?"

"Um."

I tried to ignore his question. I sucked Coke through a barber-striped plastic straw and stared out the windshield of Cade's truck.

"I'm serious," he continued. "Monica gave me five euros today. We did it right before lunch. I just want to make sure she's not taking advantage of me."

I nearly choked on my soda.

Nobody would want a girl like Monica Fassbinder to take advantage of poor Cade Hernandez.

"You can't spend euros at a 7-Eleven," I countered.

Every day, we'd stop at 7-Eleven before heading back to school for seventh-period baseball. Even though the season was over for us, we still had to show up to practice.

Also, nobody wants a truancy ticket for skipping a class that you don't have to go to.

"Well *duh*, Finn. I know that," Cade said.

"Um. Five euros is a pay raise for you, Cade."

Cade Hernandez nodded and grinned. "Oh yeah, baby."

I was simultaneously embarrassed and deeply envious of my

friend. I had never even held a girl's hand before, and suddenly I was a twenty-miles-per-second angry hornet's nest of hormones, unable to think of anything else except how I might be able to finally orchestrate an opportunity to at least talk to a girl before the earth moved another foot, another inch, through space.

Like that was ever going to happen.

:|:

SHIRTS, SKINS, FRISBEES, AND FLOUNDERS

During baseball practice that day, we played Ultimate Frisbee.

Ultimate Frisbee is kind of like football. The baseball team can get pretty rough. It's all good fun. One time, at the end of our sophomore season, I gave Blake Grunwald a bloody nose playing Ultimate Frisbee.

Blake Grunwald was a grade ahead of me and played backup catcher.

Blake Grunwald still hated me.

It was perhaps a hundred fifty million miles back, in February, I got into a fight with Blake Grunwald. Blake held on to his Ultimate Frisbee nosebleed grudge until he couldn't stand it any longer. I had never been in a real fight in my life, so it did not go very well.

Blake Grunwald freed some of my atoms.

I never said anything about it to my parents. What could they do? Boys are going to fight, no matter what.

Life goes on.

Twenty miles per second.

So, that day after lunch, Cade and I were on the "skins" team.

I usually tried to wear shirts outside because I didn't like it when people paid any attention to the emoticon scars on my back. It was different with the team, though.

Teams are like that, right?

:|:

I do not like emoticons at all. Emoticons are combinations of punctuation marks people frequently use when they don't really know how to express themselves with real words.

My emoticons are puncture-ation marks from the time a dead horse fell out of the sky onto me and my mother.

What emotion would those things express?

If I had to say what my marks meant, it would be this: *Straight-faced guy looks at his reflection in a still pond. He is not at all impressed.*

:|:

Cade Hernandez said, "What flounders look like when they fuck."

"Uh. Good one."

Cade had this game he played. Whenever I had my shirt off, he would make up some random comment about his artistic interpretation for the meaning of the scars on my back. He came up with something new every day. Like Coach Ritchey's tooth, Cade's titles for the emoticon marks on my back became a much-anticipated locker-room ritual at Burnt Mill Creek High School.

Cade Hernandez's impressions most often had something to do with sex.

Today, it was flounders.

:|:

"I don't think flounders fuck," I said.

"If I was a flounder, I would fuck," Cade said. "And it would look exactly like that."

"Uh. Of course it would, Win-Win," I said.

Cade Hernandez had seen me blank out on several occasions. One time, it happened in the boys' locker room at Burnt Mill Creek High School after a baseball game.

Being tired always elevated my chance of having a seizure.

It was the most embarrassing thing, in retrospect. It happened after our game against a team from a place called Moreno Valley.

It goes like this: I am just standing there, and first I smell something sweet—like flowers or maple syrup. Then I realize that I don't know the names for anything I am looking at. A shower-head can become a pulsating chrome anemone-thing, eating its way through the universe. *Chomp, chomp, chomp.* Sounds, colors, textures, all mash together in an enormous symphonic assault on my senses as I shrink down, smaller and smaller. I am not hot, cold, dizzy, or uncomfortable—because all of those things are *words*, which by that point in the seizure have floated away—*pfft!*—into space.

It is so beautiful.

I believe my atoms begin to drift apart—stop holding hands—in those wordless moments too.

But I see, hear, feel, taste, and smell it all.

So, after our game against Moreno Valley, I blanked out while standing under a flow of steaming water in the boys' locker-room showers.

Ridiculous.

They told me I was out for over half an hour, more than forty-five thousand miles.

That was as far as Magellan's voyage around the world.

When the words started to come back into my head and I realized what I was looking at, there were about a dozen guys around me, staring down. It looked like I was lying inside a clearing in a forest of pale, hairy legs with white Burnt Mill Creek High School locker-room towels flocking their upper branches. I saw fluorescent lights and mottled chrome showerheads above the shoulders of my teammates. I lay on my back, completely naked, on the tiles of the shower floor in a half inch of dirty water while three ambulance attendants with latex-gloved hands strategized methods for lifting me onto a perfectly white rolling gurney stretcher.

One of the paramedics was a woman. She kneeled right there beside my hip and poked an intravenous needle that was attached to a plastic bag of sugar water into my hairless arm as I lay naked on the floor of the shower.

I watched her. She stared at my penis. The atoms that built the highway of nerves in my arms were still disconnected from my brain, so I could not even move my hands to cover myself.

What a ridiculous moment it was!

When the words come back, usually the first thing I feel is anger.

The goddamned words could stay gone. It was always so pleasant, chaotic, emotionless, nameless—everything vibrating so beautifully in the universe without words.

Nobody at all knows this except for me: It is how things *really* are.

We beat Moreno Valley that day 7–2, by the way.

They were terrible!

DOORS THAT OPEN AND OPEN

My father is a writer.

He is very good at what he does, but he hates the attention it brings.

For a man who wrote novels, sacrificed the hours of his days to the invisible god of word upon word, Dad was never much of a talker. I saw how his shoulders would predictably tense and curl inward like the hood on a cobra whenever anyone got to that point of having talked too much.

Cade Hernandez, who loves to talk, could make my father turn into a cobra.

About seven years, or four billion miles, ago, my father swore he would never let anyone read another word of his writing.

Just like that, he quit.

He had written a science fiction novel called *The Lazarus Door*, which was wildly popular. The book was about, among other things, a massive religious movement—a reawakening of sorts—that occurred simultaneously with the opening of all these microscopic doors that allowed visitors from space to over-run the earth.

The visitors in his book were called incomers.

When you think about it, that would be the smartest way for creatures from way out there to get here: Blast all these mechanical doors that are no bigger than atomic dust particles out into the universe and hope they hit pay dirt. Then you open them up and send yourselves through.

In the story, most of the doors landed on shitholes, but some of them made it here.

Poof!

Pay dirt.

I liked the novel, but some people went crazy over it. I didn't find this out until after I started high school, that Dad had actually received death threats for making fun of characters from the Bible.

Imagine that.

Some people are overly sensitive about Bible stories.

When the incomers came through the little doors, they popped open—usually right in the middle of peoples' skulls and stuff, since the doors were small enough to go in your ear, or wind up under your eyelid. It was a very violent story. But the aliens looked exactly like angels—so beautiful, and completely naked with gleaming silvery-white wings.

Well, the incomers weren't angels. In fact, they liked to rape people and then eat them. Planet Earth was an endless party for the angel-aliens.

In Dad's novel, a lot of starry-eyed Christians got raped and eaten.

You'd think they'd have caught on a bit sooner!

So Dad stopped writing for publication. Everyone kept asking him when the next part of the story was going to be published.

Dad's answer, through his agent, was always this: never.

His novel sold all over the world, and they even made a movie from it too, which my father had never been able to bring himself to watch.

It's just as well. I saw it when I was thirteen. The movie was pure horseshit.

My father, whose name is Mike, wrote under the name Easton Michaels.

Easton Michaels, who wrote six novels, was an inordinately private person as a general rule.

Nobody around here knew much about us—Mike Easton and his son, Finn.

Of course, my best friend knew all about what my father did for a living, but Cade Hernandez didn't care and was generally unimpressed by all the things that most people tended to make into such monumentally big deals.

Two years after my mother was killed by a dead horse, when I was just beginning to walk again, my father married a pediatric nurse named Tracy Snow.

Tracy took care of me every day after the knackery horse turned me and my real mother into something else. I thought Nurse Snow was actually Snow White. I still call her that sometimes.

I fell in love with her.

Dad fell in love with her.

What else can you do? It all just keeps going. Twenty miles per second. Twenty miles per second.

I have a six-year-old half sister named Nadia, and we all live in a big house in San Francisquito Canyon, which is the location of one of the greatest disasters in the history of the state of California.

Not our family—a dam broke there in 1928.

Fifty billion miles ago.

Imagine that.

I met Julia Bishop the morning after Kommissar Nossik threw Cade Hernandez out of our class for asking about the punctuality of his boner.

I suppose the things that transform your life don't appear as you fancifully imagine they will. They appear as knackery trucks that carry dead horses, as collapsing dams, and maybe as beautiful girls with long dancer legs who drift silently through the dust of a California desert morning.

I had never seen anyone like her before at Burnt Mill Creek.

Anywhere, actually.

I found myself wondering how many atoms from the same calamities out there in the universe our bodies shared. I imagined that parts of my insides and parts of her insides may have come from the same exploding star, billions of years ago. Maybe my right hand and her left hand both came from the same supernova.

The atoms inside me sparked and jangled nervously as soon as I saw her.

This was new.

I rubbed my eyes.

I was ahead in credits, and a good student. And everyone in the office knew about my epilepsy, so they were always so careful around me. During third period, I worked as "Office Concierge" for Burnt Mill Creek High School. It was among my responsibilities to show visitors and new students around our campus.

I had very polite atoms.

Usually, getting a new student in May meant something bad—like the kid had been expelled from another school because of drugs or fighting.

Nobody moves in May.

The head counselor, Mrs. Hinman, tried to snap me out of my daze. She said, "Finn, this is Julia Bishop. She's starting classes today."

"Uh. Uh." I was completely dumb.

Mrs. Hinman handed me Julia Bishop's class schedule. She had an extra-concerned look on her face when she said, "Finn? Are you all right, sweetie?"

She thought I was blanking out. I knew that look. Nobody calls a sixteen-year-old guy "sweetie" unless he's pissed his pants or something.

"Oh. Sorry. Um. Hi. Here, let me show you where your classes are," I said.

Then I snatched Julia Bishop's papers and escorted her out of the office.

"Is that your name?" Julia asked.

On the south side of the office building, the stairsteps of a tiered grass field led down to an outside amphitheater and the cluster of classroom buildings that made up the campus.

I was sweating. It was hot. And something else was going on too.

"Uh. Finn. Yes," I answered.

The girl paused, studied me.

She said, "There are fish on your socks."

This is what I wore that day: red and black Burnt Mill Creek High School basketball shorts and a white sweatshirt from UCLA with the hood pulled up over the mess of my straw hair. I had gray and black skater shoes and dark blue socks with sharks swimming and swimming up around my ankles. Somehow, I felt as though I were standing there naked in front of that beautiful girl.

"Uh. Sharks." I was slack jawed, immobile and helpless, frozen in the grass. Cade had given me those socks on my sixteenth birthday, the summer before. I didn't know what else to say.

What can you say to someone like that—someone who so obviously had been paying attention to your socks?

"Well, they're cute. I like them. How tall are you?"

I went completely dumb.

Then she leaned forward and looked directly at my eyes.

"Huh! You have two different colored eyes. That's beautiful."

I couldn't help but look back at her eyes. They were brown. Julia Bishop's eyes were wondrous.

"Uh."

I squinted, trying to focus on the papers I held, the ones that would contain the mysteries of Julia Bishop.

I wondered why she'd come here—if she had parents who were monsters, or if I could find anything that might say, *This is why I ended up here on this grass staircase walking beside you, Finn.*

I smelled flowers. I prayed that it might only be her perfume.

I repeated in my head, over and over, a command for my atoms to stay here, to not blank out.

Julia Bishop.

Grade eleven.

She lived in San Francisquito Canyon.

Remember that address, Finn.

Don't walk so fast.

"Hey. I live in San Francisquito Canyon too," I said.

"Well, nice to meet you, neighbor," Julia answered.

I smell something sweet.

I struggled to come up with anything clever that would make her need to keep talking to me, looking at me and my socks, so we wouldn't have to hurry to her class. And my dumbfounded seconds ticked by.

Twenty miles.

Twenty miles.

Twenty miles.

Before I could unstick my throat, she stopped in front of me and pulled open the door to the art building.

Click!

"Well, nice socks, anyway, Finn. And eyes. You have a cool name."

"It's from Mark Twain."

Julia Bishop took her schedule from my hand.

"Why are you wearing a hood? Aren't you hot?"

I was definitely hot.

Without thinking, I put my hand on my head to see if it was true. I was, in fact, wearing a hood. I was also unaware of just about anything in the universe that wasn't named Julia Bishop.

I pulled the hood down. My hair was a mess. Some of it fell across my eye. I refused to blink.

I only stared at her. I realized, relieved, that what I smelled on the air must have been atoms from the perfume on her neck floating across the gap between us, because Finn Easton would have been on his back and staring out at the wordless universe by now if he were having a seizure.

And Julia Bishop said, "I'm not flirting with you, you know."

"I didn't think you were," I said.

"I'm not," she said.

The door shut.

She disappeared inside.

Six foot one, I mouthed. No sounds came out.

Eventually, staring at the shut door, I got my lower jaw to rejoin the upper.

SPACE DOGS AND BULLFIGHTERS

My dog enjoys rolling around in dead things. Her name is Laika.

Laika was named for the dog who died in space.

I have always been somewhat obsessed with that unfortunate animal.

When she slept outside, which is what we made her do whenever she rolled in dead things and then returned home stinking with a guilty canine grin on her snout, Laika was exiled to a small plastic cube with a barred chrome door that made it look like an old jail cell.

I penned "*Sputnik 2*" and drew the ringed planet Saturn, stars, and comets on the outside of Laika's crate.

Almost nobody gets the joke.

There is more room for my little dog inside her plastic crate than there was inside *Sputnik 2* for the original Laika.

Laika means "barker" in Russian.

At least *my* Laika lives through her *Sputnik* experience. The original Laika, as most accepted theories go, died about five hours into her spaceflight when the internal temperature of *Sputnik 2* began to rise sharply and the satellite lost communication with the planet of humans and dogs. Nobody really knew what Laika was doing up there, besides getting uncomfortably hot.

For all that the scientists down here on Planet Earth knew, she could have been singing "Ninety-Nine Bottles of Beer on the Wall" to herself over and over and over.

Not a very cheerful voyage.

But the satellite stayed in orbit for more than five months after that—a lonely and most certainly dead dog circling and circling overhead while the earth traveled about 240 million miles through space. Eventually, Laika and her spacecraft were incinerated when their orbit decayed in April 1958.

She was definitely dead after that happened.

Laika's fourteen-billion-year-old atoms were free again.

I believe many of those atoms found their way into my corpse-loving rat terrier—possibly into me as well.

The knackery never shuts down.

After that first day, I did not manage to catch a glimpse of Julia Bishop for the rest of the week.

Thinking about Julia Bishop made me crazy. I found myself considering doing things I would never have thought possible: waiting for her outside classroom doors or taking a walk up the canyon to see where her home was.

I didn't have the nerve.

I did not say anything to Cade Hernandez about meeting Julia Bishop.

What could I say, anyway? That I had fallen in love with a

ANDREW SMITH

girl I didn't even know, just because she admired the socks I was wearing? That she actually noticed my eyes?

That was ridiculous.

But I had never felt so messed up on the inside. I imagined myself as some kind of hero who could overcome all his self-doubt and do something absurd like ask Julia Bishop, since she was practically my next-door neighbor, if she would like to come over to my house and visit, or maybe look at my socks, or do the kind of shit that normal kids do.

But I knew there was not the slightest chance of that happening.

I didn't know what normal kids did in these situations.

If I asked Cade what I should do about Julia Bishop, he would ruin everything. It would be innocent enough—just Cade being Cade—but it would happen as inevitably as the pull of gravity.

I couldn't let that happen.

So Cade and I drove quietly to school the morning after I met her. We stopped at Coffee Kiosk and bought coffees with sugar and cream, and we drank them in the student parking lot at Burnt Mill Creek High School while everything kept moving, twenty miles per second, twenty miles per second.

My *actual* next-door neighbor in San Francisquito Canyon was a very old man named Manny Castellan.

Manny Castellan was seventy-three years old. That's an awful lot of miles through space. His atoms were probably getting very tired of holding on to one another.

We lived on four acres. Most of the homes in the canyon had enough land to keep horses. Manny's house had stables, but they were empty. Our place had a pool, a gazebo, and an entire guest house.

Dad's imagination paid all the bills we ever had.

We lived well.

Manny was from Mexico. His real name was Manuel.

Manuel Castellan used to be a bullfighter in Mexico, forty years ago and about twenty-five billion miles away from here. He complained to me once that modern people had generally lost their respect for the art of bullfighting.

He told me his bullfighter name was Manolito.

I thought it would be cool to have a bullfighter name.

One time I said, "What do you think *my* bullfighter name would be, assuming I ever fought with a bull?"

Mr. Castellan studied me thoughtfully. He looked me up and down as though he were receiving some signal from out there, somewhere.

He said, "I would call you Caballito."

"What is that?"

"*Caballito* is a little horse."

"I am not little," I argued.

"You are for a horse," Manuel Castellan said.

I nodded.

I wrote down what Manuel Castellan told me. Sometimes I carried a small red moleskine journal in my pocket.

He asked, "Why are you writing that down?"

I said, "I never get to talk to bullfighters."

"Bullfighting is dead," Manuel Castellan said.

Good for the bulls.

I asked Mr. Castellan what they did with the losers of the

match, if they were rendered into useful products like explosives, or lubricants on condoms.

Manuel Castellan asked me, "What are condoms?"

I had to tell him what condoms are. It wasn't embarrassing, and the bullfighter was fascinated by my description of how condoms worked. Then he asked if I had one I could show him, and I told him no.

Why would I ever need a condom?

The bullfighter said, "You never know, Caballito."

Manuel Castellan told me the dead bulls were dragged away and their meat was sold in butcher shops. Dead, tormented bulls produced a very popular meat.

Who knew?

They could have thrown them from bridges for all I knew.

THE POLITICS OF TEENAGE GRUDGES

At the end of the school week—the week of Nazi Day and Julia Bishop—Cade Hernandez brought a suitcase filled with his belongings to my house in San Francisquito Canyon.

My parents and sister were leaving to spend five days in New York City without me.

I pouted to Mom and Dad, "I never get to go anywhere."

As soon as I'd said it I calculated the worthlessness of this autopilot adolescent protest.

Tracy said, "What about that trip you have planned to visit Dunston University with Cade this summer?"

If Cade didn't get drafted into the big leagues in his senior year, we had plans on going to college together, and Dunston was the place. Dunston University was a private school in Oklahoma, with a top-notch baseball program and one of the nation's best liberal arts schools.

"That doesn't count. It's a school."

"I'm sure you and Cade will manage to turn the next five days into a vacation filled with debauchery and vice," my dad countered.

He probably had a point.

I nodded. Mom and Dad exchanged concerned and mature glances.

Cade Hernandez was going to be my babysitter.

Nadia, my sister, was on school break, and I had to stay home, since my school year was not over yet. But my parents allowed Cade to live there with me during that time, despite Dad's reservations about my friend. They knew Cade could keep an eye on their epileptic boy, but I thought it was all part of the master plan to ensure Finn Easton's atoms would never escape the state of California.

Dad had to go to New York for work.

I had bunk beds in my room.

I believe the idea behind them had something to do with an expectation that I was to conjure some kind of invisible little brother, a playmate, because I never understood why Tracy— Mom—stubbornly clung to the aesthetic notion that boy plus bedroom equaled bunk beds, while my sister's room was designed like a perfumed pillow palace.

Nadia was the princess of San Francisquito Canyon.

Cade was asleep in the lower bunk when I woke up on Saturday morning. I never slept in the bottom bed because it made me feel like frozen food—all closed in and boxed away in the dark.

Cade was pressing a pillow across his head with the bend of his arm.

Cade Hernandez was an expert sleeper.

I pulled a T-shirt on over my bare chest and went downstairs. The sun was not up past the rim of the canyon behind our house, but it was already sweltering hot. Most of the time, wearing shirts was a habit of mine.

I didn't like it when anyone paid too much attention to the emoticon scars on my back.

:|:

My father and I drank coffee together outside on our patio every Saturday morning, even during winter storms.

It was what we did.

A cup of coffee with my dad usually lasted about forty thousand miles, maybe fewer this Saturday since Mom was hurriedly finishing the family's New York packing job.

Dad stared and stared at me.

It wasn't the way Cade Hernandez stared. There was no messing-with-you intent from my father. I knew what it was.

Dad was afraid that, like my *real* mother, one day I would be gone.

Poof!

"Laika stinks," he said.

My dog sat up in front of my bare feet, beneath the metal table where Dad and I drank our Saturday coffee.

I sipped and nodded. "I shall prepare the tub of horror."

Laika, knowing the phrase, clenched herself into a tightened armadillo.

Laika's tub of horror was a plastic toddler's wading pool, blue, and decorated with a frieze of press-formed dolphins, starfish, and bubbles dancing around its outer wall.

Such horror.

Dad leaned toward me and said, "It looks like it's about time you started shaving."

For some reason, *that* was embarrassing. I could talk in specific detail with the bullfighter about how condoms are used, but the minute my father started noticing the effects of puberty on me I began to choke and sweat.

I felt myself turning red.

"Shaving *what?*" I said.

Dad tilted his head. "I can see something."

"Maybe I need to wash my face."

I was one-point-seven million miles away, two months, from my seventeenth birthday, and if I weren't so tall, I could probably pass for a sixth-grader.

Dad relaxed. Then he recited his laundry list of instructions: where he'd left the contact information for his hotel, where I could find money if I needed it, not to forget to charge my phone and have it with me at all times, that trash day was Wednesday, and not to get into Cade Hernandez's truck if Cade was drinking alcohol.

"We don't drink, Dad."

That was almost fifty percent of the truth.

Well, not really so much as that.

"Finn. I was sixteen once too."

"That was about fourteen billion miles back that way," I argued.

Distance was more important than time to my father, too. That was why he was so afraid that I would go away someday.

"Okay," he said.

"Okay," I agreed.

Then I said this: "Dad, I've been bothered about something somebody said to me a few days ago."

"Something somebody said," my father repeated, making sure to stress each "some."

Dad did not appreciate the vagueness of teenage communication.

"It was a girl."

"A girl?" Dad was positively enthusiastic.

"A carrier of twin X chromosomes," I affirmed.

"Well?"

I took another sip from my coffee and said, "She said this: 'I'm not flirting with you, you know.'"

My father nodded thoughtfully.

"What does that even mean, Dad?" I asked.

"She was flirting with you, Finn. Definitely."

"That's what I thought too."

I loved my father more than anything.

Cade was just coming out of the bedroom when I got upstairs.

He rubbed his eyes and yawned while he clutched one hand over his crotch. Cade went into the bathroom and peed loudly. I'd noticed the protrusion below his lip that meant he was already chewing tobacco too.

Breakfast of champions.

And from inside my bathroom, Cade announced, "Peeing with a boner is so fucking ridiculous, man."

"Wow," I said. "Just . . . wow."

I shook my head.

"Really," Cade said.

He pulled the door open, then turned and dropped a stringy brown glob of spit into the unflushed toilet.

I pointed at my friend's mouth. "Dude. You'll have to get rid of that shit. My parents are still here."

Cade said, "Oh."

He extracted a black wad of tobacco from his lower lip and—*splash!*—dropped it into his stew of piss and saliva in the toilet.

Then Cade looked at me with a serious eye and said, "And, Finn: Don't try to tell me you didn't know that peeing with a boner is a painful fucking nightmare."

I shook my head.

Cade flushed the toilet.

He said, "It's ridiculous. I should ask Mr. Nossik about it."

Cade Hernandez was going to kill that man.

After the Jeep was packed, we stood barefoot in the driveway and said our good-byes.

Mom and Nadia kissed me. They waved and smiled at Cade. I believed they both actually *wanted* to kiss Cade Hernandez, because all girls seemed to want to kiss him, but that would have been far too much for my father to handle.

So Mom and Nadia got into the Jeep and waited for my dad.

Dad reissued his usual string of father-to-teenage-son admonitions about what Cade and I should not do while he was gone. And, as was his usual custom just before getting into the Jeep and driving off, he held my shoulders and looked directly into my eyes, plumbing the depths of the stuff that was back there as though he could see whether or not a seizure was coming anytime soon.

"I love you, son."

"Love you, Dad."

And, dutifully, I bent down so he could kiss my forehead.

That was how it always went.

We would eventually end up at Blake Grunwald's house that night.

Blake Grunwald was having a party.

It was a night of the moon in perigee, and it was the night when I finally got to talk to Julia Bishop, the girl who lived a half mile up the canyon from my home.

I had a seizure that night too.

It was a ridiculous night, as Cade Hernandez might say, because we would not normally have been welcomed at Blake Grunwald's party. Blake Grunwald hated us both. To be honest, Blake hated me more, but he hated Cade by association since we were best friends.

Blake only asked us in because we had girls with us.

The politics of teenage grudges are very complex.

MY NEIGHBOR JULIA

Cade and I spent the afternoon swimming in my pool.

We lay stretched out like lazy seals on wet towels to sun our-selves on the deck while we drank Mountain Dew. When Cade finished, he used his empty bottle as a spittoon.

It was like we owned the place and could do whatever we wanted to do, which in Cade's case involved chewing tobacco all day long, at least until he had to report to work at Flat Face Pizza.

"Monica Fassbinder's split-finger grip," Cade announced.

"Huh?"

Cade Hernandez poked his index finger into the center of my back.

:|:

"Oh. Uh. Good one. You're really gross, Win-Win," I said.

Cade spit. The green plastic bottle was one-third full of black goo.

"She's got talented hands," Cade said.

"I never noticed."

"It pays for my habit, Finn."

"It's disgusting."

"You're just jealous."

"Maybe," I said. "I don't think I'd ever have the guts to let someone give me a hand job in a custodian's shed during school."

Cade spit again. "She did it to me other places too. In my truck. One time she did it to me in the dugout at Pioneer Field."

I groaned. "Dude. In your truck? Where I sit? And I sit in that dugout, too."

Cade shrugged. "We all do."

Cade tried to talk me into hanging out at Flat Face Pizza and waiting for him while he worked. He said it would be fun.

I told him that it sure sounded like fun but I'd rather pull all my toenails out with red-hot needle-nose pliers.

Fun.

"I'm okay. It's not like I'm afraid of being home alone," I said.

:|:

So Cade took a shower upstairs and changed into his Flat Face Pizza delivery-boy uniform, which was just a T-shirt with the childish Flat Face logo and a pair of blue jeans. He promised to bring back some pizza for dinner when he was off work, which wouldn't be until eleven.

Late supper.

We could do whatever we wanted for nearly an entire week. Well, to be honest, five days is almost nine million miles.

But almost as soon as Cade pulled his truck out from our driveway, I smelled it.

The flowers had come back for another unexpected visit.

It was ridiculous.

I stood there in front of my house, wearing nothing but a pair of white swim trunks, and as soon as the smell hit me, I knew what was about to happen.

So I desperately tried to trap all the words inside my head. Cade drove off.

It was a helpless situation.

I did not want to suffer the embarrassment of blanking out in broad daylight, nearly naked as I was, on the grass of my front yard.

I spun around and stumbled toward the door, but despite my will it felt as though everything of Finn from the knees down had already begun to fizzle away.

Atoms will drift apart and get rearranged in the great knackery of the universe.

House.

Door.

Latch.

Steps.

Caballito.

All those words.

Poof!

I fell through the doorway and into another universe that was not my home. But I saw this: Across the room, on the raised step leading toward our kitchen, stood two little girls. Blond-white hair cut in perfect bowls at the bottoms of their earlobes. One of them was maybe seven, and the other, five—little dresses, and white socks pulled up and folded just below their knees.

I dimly remember propping myself up, horselike on all fours, staring down at the swirling patterns in the cool wood of the living room floor. Swirling and swirling. *And what is this? And what is this?*

Then everything was suddenly gone. All the words poured out of me, a supernova of nouns and verbs, the containers of everything, now nameless, now just *there*.

This is the universe at twenty miles per second.

It is a very beautiful thing.

:|:

I pissed myself.

I'd left the door wide open and it was night.

I knew only those three things when the words started to trickle back: I pissed myself, it was dark, and I was staring out at the rest of the world on the other side of an open door.

Goddamn, the words come back at their own speed, and some of them manage to get very far away from Finn Easton.

Piss.

Floor.

Door.

Night.

My entire body shook, like the epileptic boy was attached to live electrodes.

Nothing was connected. I had to wait until the words

ANDREW SMITH

sluggishly came back, till I could smell the ammonia stink of the urine puddled around me on the floor, feel the stinging burn in my crotch, staring and staring out the door until all things reclaimed their names and I knew where I was.

Then I became so angry.

Anyone at all could simply have walked into my house, done whatever they wanted to do. But who would want to do anything in a house where some twitching zombie kid is lying facedown in a pool of his piss?

There was something on my right arm.

The atoms in my nerves reconnected, and I could feel Laika pressed against me. My dog always did that when I blanked out. She must have found a dry spot on the shores of Lake Finn where she could keep an eye on me.

I was mad.

"Get the fuck away from me!" I snapped.

Laika curled up, dejected, and shivered away from me to a corner of the living room, watching, watching.

Later I would feel bad about such things, but when I came back from blanking out, I acted so horribly. I swore at people, even if I loved them.

I hated that about myself.

I can't say how long I stayed there on the floor trying to decide if I should shut the door first, or wipe up my piss, or get out of my goddamned swim trunks and rinse myself off beneath a shower. That's how things always were: I could not make those connector places in my brain tell me what to do.

I may have been there for no more than a hundred sideways

miles, or it may have been a hundred thousand.

Twenty miles.

Twenty miles.

I was so disgusted with myself.

And I knew my parents and sister were not there, but I couldn't remember what had happened to them.

Imagine that.

I hadn't moved at all, just kept my eyes pinned to the light/dark band of roadway that eventually became named San Francisquito Canyon.

And from somewhere down near my disconnected feet, there came this: "Are you okay? Did you take drugs or something? Can you hear me?"

I pivoted my chin along the floor so I could see where the voice came from.

Julia Bishop sat on the floor beside my feet, cross-legged along the shores of Lake Finn. She held a phone in her hand.

"I was about to call nine-one-one. Are you okay?" she said.

"I—no. Fuck no!"

I had such a foul mouth at these times.

I could have died from embarrassment. This was the worst possible situation.

It was so ridiculous.

"What are you fucking doing here?" I demanded.

What an idiot I was! Not only was I lying there practically naked in my own piss, but I was acting like a complete asshole to the most beautiful girl in the universe. And, worst of all, I had a very stiff hard-on.

Julia Bishop was obviously embarrassed. I had managed to pass some of my shit off onto her.

What a hero.

"Look," I said. "I. Uh. Don't look at me. Don't pay attention to me. I apologize for swearing. This happens to me. I can't control what I say or do sometimes. I'm a fucking epileptic."

The words choked in my throat.

I wanted to die.

"I'm sorry," Julia said. "I was just walking past. I heard your dog howling, and the door was wide open. I'm so sorry. I tried to see if there was someone here."

"Fuck this," I said.

"Do you want me to call someone?"

"No."

I realized she must have been looking at me.

She had to have seen *everything*.

:|:

It was terrible. I was wearing nothing more than thin, wet swim trunks, lying face down on top of a painfully rigid erection. That was something that frequently happened when I blanked out.

Who would guess death was such an endless turn-on?

"Can I help you? You're shivering," she said.

"You can shut my fucking door."

And as soon as Julia Bishop stood and moved toward the front door, I forced myself up, dizzy and dripping, my shaking hands covering my stiff penis, and I ran upstairs to the shower.

Ridiculous.

PIZZA-DELIVERY BOY

Julia Bishop stayed in my house and waited while I took a shower.

I felt terrible for how I'd acted.

After I get mad about my blanking out, I get depressed. I can't help it. It happens every time.

The depression can be pretty bad sometimes too. I was particularly sad that night after Julia Bishop walked in and found me lying on my living room floor.

But I never tell anyone about feeling this way, because I am so good at just being fine.

:|:

Most times when I'd feel mopey after coming back from a seizure, I would find myself trying to remember my mother, thinking about how that dead horse fell one hundred sideways miles to land—*thud!*—directly on top of us.

I generally considered how nice it would be if I could simply stop myself from hurtling through space so fast, if only for a few seconds at a time.

If I could have done such a thing, that horse would have been halfway to Sacramento by the time it landed.

Was I sorry for what happened? Sure I was, but that was billions of miles away from here. And if there is one thing I am certain of, it is this: When we think about all those miles in back of us, it's easy to feel regret—sometimes because of things we didn't do, sometimes for the things we did.

Or we feel regret because of what happened to us, since we're all so goddamned innocent and undeserving.

And when we think about the miles ahead, we worry about something that probably isn't ever going to happen anyway.

Imagine that.

Worry and regret are both useless weights that provide no drag. They never did anything to slow down the planet for one goddamned second.

My atoms have been around for fourteen billion years. I know beyond any doubt they have seen far worse things than a dead horse falling out of the sky.

It doesn't mean I don't cry about it once in a while.

That's okay, right?

I didn't bring any clean clothes into the bathroom to put on.

My wet swim trunks hung across the top of the shower door. I was terrified to step into the openness of the house, and I wanted to sleep.

So I sat on the toilet, wrapped in a towel. My head ached, and I was terribly sad.

I put my face in my hands. My wet hair hung down, *drip-drip-drip*ping onto my lap.

Hair grows about half an inch per month, the same amount of time it takes us to fly fifty million miles through space.

I'll admit this: I think about ways to kill myself.

Do I need to be specific?

Everybody thinks about it, right?

I am not afraid to contemplate such things, but I am afraid of what suicide would do to my dad, to Cade, or Mom and Nadia.

They are the anchors that keep me from knackering my fourteen-billion-year-old atoms back out into the universe where they came from, where they belong.

Dad would be so mad at me if he ever found out what happened.

:|:

I don't know how long I sat there with my face in my hands—maybe ten thousand miles—until I finally gave up on the idea of hiding away in my bathroom forever.

Not very much hair grew.

I got up, wiped my face, and came out, wrapped in a towel.

I called down from the top of the stairs, "Are you still here?"

Then Julia Bishop appeared below.

She was looking at me.

"I thought you knew my name. It's Julia," she said.

"I know that."

"I wasn't sure if you needed help or anything," Julia said.

"I'm really sorry for how I acted, um, Julia." I felt myself turning red, backing away from the upstairs railing, unable to stop looking at her, wishing she wouldn't look at *me*. I shook my head apologetically. "I'm not very nice. I'm sorry."

"It's okay, Finn. Really. I . . . um. I cleaned up your floor."

I was horrified.

"Why?"

But before Julia Bishop could answer me, the front door swung open and Cade Hernandez, awkwardly carrying two Flat Face Pizza boxes in one hand, jangling car keys and a paper sack containing what I clearly saw to be at least two twelve-packs of beer in the other, came into the house.

Monica Fassbinder was right behind him, hanging on to his elbow.

Cade and Monica looked up at me as I stood at the top of the stairs, naked except for a damp bath towel wrapped around my hips. Then Cade glanced at Julia Bishop before he looked back at me one more time.

He was chewing tobacco. I could see it growing like desert tumbleweeds below the teeth that showed in Cade's astonished grin.

Cade Hernandez nearly dropped his pizza boxes and sack of beer.

He was very drunk.

Twenty miles.

Monica Fassbinder said, "Oh. Ha ha! Oops, Finn."

Twenty miles.

And Cade said, "Holy fucking shit, Finn! You better have used a condom!"

Ridiculous.

I could have died on the spot.

What else could possibly have gone wrong?

I threw my hands up in defeat and said, "Cade Hernandez, Monica Fassbinder: Meet Julia Bishop, my new neighbor. Julia: This is Cade, my best friend. He's staying here for the next five days, trying to kill me with embarrassment while my parents are in New York, and this is his . . . um . . . girlfriend, Monica. Why don't you all chat amongst yourselves while I go and change into something that isn't quite so *fucking naked*?"

And with that, I backed away from the railing and shut myself inside my bedroom.

Slam!

I did not get dressed.

Inside my room, in the dark, my towel and I climbed up onto my bed, and I lay there with a pillow over my face.

I could easily have started to cry; I was acting like such a baby.

But I just wanted everything to disappear, to drift away into namelessness again, and then stay that way for another fourteen billion years.

And I did not intend to go back downstairs either. I lay there imagining all the terrible things Cade Hernandez might be saying or doing to ensure the complete ruination of any chance I might ever have at finding a normal, decent friend who also happened to be a beautiful girl.

What was I thinking?

Eventually—who knew how many miles it was—the door opened and the light flicked on.

"Leave me the fuck alone," I said.

"You okay, Finn?"

"I got a headache."

"Dude."

"What?"

"That girl."

"What did she say?"

"She didn't say nothing, Finn."

"Sure she didn't."

I felt Cade lean against the top bunk, beside my knees. Even with my pillow pressed over my face, I could smell the booze on him, the atoms from what he'd been getting drunk on wheezing out into the universe with each breath Cade Hernandez exhaled.

"You . . . uh . . . did that thing, didn't you?"

Cade Hernandez knew I blanked out.

"Yes. I did my fucking thing, Cade."

"Um. Your dad made me promise I would call him if it happened. What time is it in New York?"

"Here plus three," I said.

Cade answered, "You and your fucking math."

"Oh, yeah? Well, fuck you, too, Win-Win. And as long as you're going to call my dad, just pass the phone over to me, because he made *me* promise I'd call him if you ever got drunk."

"Fuck that. I ain't calling, Finn. I wouldn't do that."

"Sorry."

"Dude."

"What?"

"That girl."

"I know."

WILLIAM MULHOLLAND'S SELF-TAUGHT MISTAKE

Cade Hernandez could talk me into doing just about anything.

He said, "Dude. Come downstairs with us and have some fun. But put some clothes on first. I can see your balls."

I made him stay in my room with me while I got dressed. There was no way I'd go downstairs by myself and make some kind of pathetic entrance like a freak in a sideshow.

Step right up! Come see the epileptic boy!

So I climbed down from bed and pulled on some shorts and a tank top. I slipped my bare feet into a new pair of tennis shoes Dad had given me the week before, and I followed Cade Hernandez out of my room to face my audience.

My dog waited for me in the hallway.

When she saw me, Laika curled up into a little ball and watched me with guilty dog eyes.

"You're so dumb," I said. But she squirmed happily when I bent down so I could scratch behind her ears.

Laika had wild and sudden emotional swings.

That's my dog.

. . .

When we got downstairs, Cade announced, "He fell asleep. I had to wake him up."

The girls sat on the living room couch. Monica drank a beer and pretended to be checking something important on her cell phone.

Monica Fassbinder had a permanently distracted look in her eyes, like nothing could possibly happen fast enough for that girl. I wondered if she would have been pleased at forty miles per second.

And I also wondered if she got text messages in German. I planned to ask her about it one day.

One of the pizza boxes lay with its lid folded back on our coffee table.

Maybe it was my own personal hang-up, but I felt like both girls were waiting to see if I would flip out or something.

"I'm okay," I said.

:|:

I sat down on the floor across from Julia. I couldn't help but scan the living room to see if it was true that she'd actually cleaned up after me. She caught me looking for it too.

The floor was completely dry and spotless.

Why would anyone do something like that?

I wasn't even nice to her at all.

I pursed my lips straight and nodded at her. I would have said thank you, but it was too embarrassing.

Cade Hernandez opened his can of chewing tobacco and pushed a fresh wad of the stuff down behind his lower lip. Here was a kid who could actually chew tobacco *and* drink beer at the same time.

That was complex modern multitasking for a high school athlete.

Julia and I ate pizza. Cade offered Julia a beer, but she told him no.

He started to pass one in my direction, but I raised my hand and shook my head. I couldn't drink a beer after blanking out. It would kill me.

Cade and I had gotten drunk together in the past.

It was fun. Cade had taught me how to do it. The first time we'd gotten drunk together, we were fourteen years old. I passed out at Cade's house and we missed school the next morning. Dad grounded me and took away my cell phone for two weeks, but he never found out I'd been drinking. I told him Cade and I had been playing video games.

Imagine that.

Cade spit into an empty can and said, "We're going to a party at Blake Grunwald's house. His parents are in Vegas."

I looked at Cade in disbelief.

"Blake invited us to his house?"

"Well, he said we could come as long as we brought girls and beer. We might be out of beer by the time we get there, but at least we have some girls. Blake and his friends . . . you know—they're total losers. The place is like a fucking locker room—all guys. All ballplayers. Well, there's some girls, but they're ugly enough to be guys. But lots of booze, Finn."

"You were there?" I asked.

"Delivered pizza." Cade spit and opened another beer. Then

he laughed. "You should have seen what me and Monica did to that dickhead's pizza."

I looked at Monica. She had a bored and confused look on her face that said she didn't really *get* the stuff we American boys joked about, and why we thought certain things were such big deals. I believed it was Monica's act.

Cade silently mouthed *five dollars* to me and pointed at the pizza.

He laughed.

I suddenly lost my appetite.

I said, "Well, you are *not* going to drive anywhere. You're drunk. And so's Monica."

Cade slid his keys across the coffee table. They landed on the floor beside my knee. Cade had taught me how to drive, too.

I was horrible!

My dad would have a stroke if he knew I'd driven Cade's truck before; and driving right after a seizure was definitely a dangerous idea. One time, I'd crashed Cade's truck into somebody's mailbox. Cade Hernandez thought it was hilarious. I still felt guilty over bending the mailbox.

Someone had to be the grown-up, I thought.

"Oh, yeah. Right," I said. "If you drive, we end up in jail, and if I drive, we end up in the hospital. Lose-lose, Win-Win."

Then Julia said, "I have a car. I can drive."

So the four of us started off, walking toward Julia Bishop's house. Actually, it was five, counting Laika.

We crossed the road and followed the creekbed north.

In May, there was no water in San Francisquito Creek, just a few spots where puddles had been trapped in some of the deeper depressions of the bed.

Cade and Monica followed slowly at a distance, like twin satellites being pulled along by the gravity of Julia Bishop and me. I'd turn around from time to time and catch one of them opening another beer. Once, I saw Cade pissing into the brush.

On the way up the canyon, Julia Bishop told me she'd come out only to look at the moon. She said the moon was in perigee that night, the closest it got to the planet of humans and dogs.

"So," I said, "were you just going for a walk to see the moon, or were you honestly trying to meet your epileptic neighbor?"

Julia Bishop was a good subject-changer. "Did you know this is the second brightest moon tonight in more than a century?"

"Is that right?" I said.

"Yes."

"Then you could see it from anywhere," I pointed out.

"Okay, then," Julia admitted, "I heard you lived in that big house. I wanted to see."

"Um," I said.

I cleared my throat and toe-kicked a rock. "You didn't get a chance to answer my question before. Why did you do that—clean up after me, I mean? You didn't have to do something like that."

"I felt bad for you. You were so sad, and I thought you were just scared," Julia said.

"But that was, um . . . pretty disgusting, what I did," I said.

"It was no big deal. I've done it before."

"What? Cleaned up a sixteen-year-old kid's pee?" I said.

"Well, no. But I've changed a baby's diaper," she said.

"Wow," I said. "A diaper. That really makes me feel like killing myself right about now."

Then she laughed and touched my arm.

She said, "Forget about it."

I said, "Well, sorry. And thank you for what you did, Julia."

Cade and Monica weren't paying attention to us at all.

Laika had run off somewhere into the dry wash of the canyon.

While the earth travels twenty miles per second, it pulls the moon with it through space. And the moon, dragged along, trudges around us at a little more than half a mile per second.

The moon is slow.

It is the hair of the earth.

"Compared with us, the moon moves like a glacier in space," I said.

There has never been a shortage of dead things in San Francisquito Canyon.

Julia Bishop had no idea. There were hundreds of accounts of ghosts wandering the canyon at night. I do not believe in ghosts, unless they are just lingering atoms from the dead; atoms that didn't know how to let go of one another.

So I told her about William Mulholland, who was a self-taught civil engineer.

Self-taught civil engineers are probably as trustworthy as self-taught brain surgeons and self-taught airline pilots.

Like sexual confusion and atom bombs, self-taught civil engineers are causally associated with extinction.

William Mulholland built a concrete dam in San Francisquito

Canyon in 1926. The dam was called the St. Francis Dam, and it filled the canyon with a massive reservoir.

Twelve billion gallons.

At that time, it was approximately six gallons of water—about fifty pounds' worth—for every human being alive on the planet.

In 1928, William Mulholland's dam collapsed, releasing a one-hundred-forty-foot wall of water and tumbling chunks of concrete as big as locomotives. Twelve billion gallons of water suddenly decided to make a run for the Pacific Ocean, which is about fifty miles from here.

Nobody knows for certain how many people died in the disaster. Many estimates place the number of dead at around five hundred.

Bodies washed ashore as far away as coastal Mexico.

Our homes were built along the same channel where countless corpses were dragged and pummeled by William Mulholland's self-taught mistake.

The knackery never shuts down.

ONE ATOM AT A TIME

Laika found a dead coyote. The thing lay decaying in the knackery of San Francisquito Canyon's creekbed.

"Something fucking stinks," Cade announced.

Monica Fassbinder pecked at her cell phone. She had a distracted and bored *are-we-there-yet* look on her face.

The moon was full and bright enough that I found the mangled coyote between clumps of wild blooming buckwheat, where some other creature had likely dragged it. Its side had been laid wide open, and in the white-hot light from the moon, I could see bones and the fetid yellow coils of rotting innards. The coyote had probably been hit by a car on the highway and then limped out here into the middle of the wash to lie down and die.

When I found her, Laika was joyously wriggling on the mat of the carcass, all four of her little paws, dancing, pointed up at the moon and stars.

The atoms that disengaged from the dead coyote smelled worse than anything imaginable. I had to lift the neckline of my tank top to cover my mouth and nose, just to get within ten feet of the thing.

"You're so stupid!" I said. "I hate you so much."

Which was true. At that moment, I really did hate my dog.

I have wild mood swings too.

Laika, busted and guilty, rolled away from the mattress of her newfound, dead friend. She curled her tail between her legs, grinned with toothy contrition, and presented her belly at my feet.

"I'm not touching you! Go away! Get in your cage!" I said.

Laika knew what to do. She ran for home. I would find her curled up inside her little spaceship when I went back.

"Aww . . . poor thing," Julia said.

I pulled my shirt down from my face and moved away from the stink of the carcass.

"My dog is dumb. She rolls in dead things."

"Maybe it's easier to catch up to dead things. They don't go so fast," Julia said.

"Everything moves at the same speed, living or dead," I answered. "Twenty miles per second."

"Oh. Sure."

"It's easy to figure out. Pi. The distance to the sun. Three hundred and sixty-five days. It comes out to twenty miles per second, give or take a bit."

"Oh, yeah," she said, "that sounds real easy."

"Are you messing with me?"

"I'm not trying to."

"Dude. Julia. How far away *is* your house?" Cade said.

Julia pointed to a light on the west side of the canyon.

"It's right there," she said.

"I hope you guys have a four-wheel drive or something," I said.

"I realized I bought the wrong kind of car for living here," Julia said.

There were only a few homes on the west side of the canyon. In winter, when the flooding came, residents there would have to drive through the creek, which became impassable during heavy rainfall. Frequently, the people on the west bank would have to leave their cars along the shoulder of the highway and try to wade across the raging creek just to get to their homes.

During a couple of the worst seasons, Dad and Mom actually took in what they called West Bank refugees who could not get to their homes. My mom and dad fed the stranded neighbors and allowed them to sleep in our house.

There were no bridges here. I think people in the canyon pretty much gave up on the idea of civil engineering.

"Well, it really stinks here. If we're going to look at the second brightest moon in one hundred years, we should probably move away from dead things," I said.

"A century is about sixty billion miles," I said.

Julia Bishop was sixteen years old. Her skin was dark and smooth, and she had the most perfectly curved slender legs. I tried to devise some strategy that might allow me to casually touch them, just like Julia had touched my arm.

The thought made my atoms feel very alive and aroused, not nearly like the fourteen-billion-year-old sourpusses I was used to.

I was certain I'd never feel anything as flawless as Julia Bishop's skin.

But I was too afraid.

We sat on the ground with our knees bent, at the edge of Julia's yard. From our spot in a clearing between some dried Lydia brooms and spiny mesquite brush, we watched the moon as it rose higher into the sky above the canyon rim.

"Oh," Julia said, "I can't even imagine what sixty billion *anythings* would look like."

I thought about it.

"Neither can I," I said.

Cade and Monica sat away from us, drinking. Cade had his arm around Monica, and occasionally I could hear the wet sounds of their kissing. I didn't really *get* their relationship at all. Cade was athletic, smart, energetic, and high maintenance; Monica was quiet, brooding, and dissatisfied. Monica's wardrobe came in one color: black. And she only listened to bands like the Smiths and the Cure. As far as I could tell, Cade and Monica had only one thing in common.

It was a miracle they were still conscious, too. And they fully intended to have Julia drive us to Blake Grunwald's party, where they would certainly drink more alcohol.

That's what kids do.

"Not many people change schools in May," I said. "Where did you come from?"

Julia smiled. She was startlingly beautiful. I looked directly into her eyes and saw tiny moons floating in them.

Twenty miles.

Twenty miles.

Then she said, "I came from up there."

Julia Bishop nodded toward the moon and stars.

I said, "Oh, yeah. Well, you know, I guess we all did."

"No." Julia said, "I mean I came through a Lazarus Door, just like you."

"Oh," I said. It was a groan, actually.

Lazarus Doors.

This is the truth: In the book my father wrote, *The Lazarus Door*, the tiny, atom-size particles the angel-aliens came through to arrive at the endless orgy and dinner table of Planet Earth were called Lazarus Doors.

"You read that book too?" I said.

"Hasn't everyone?" Julia asked.

Cade Hernandez, now animated and enthusiastic, said, "I never read books. Sorry, Finner."

Then he burped and laughed.

Monica Fassbinder said, "What book?"

Here is another truth: My father once said to me that sometimes the smallest thing—a Lazarus Door–size idea—can force an entire book to squeeze out through it.

Poof!

I believed this.

My father told me the inspiration for his book came from the scar on my back.

:|:

Imagine that.

Once they got here, the incomers from Dad's novel decided to surgically remove their wings, in order to blend in better with human beings.

Human beings were not very smart. We never have been, to be honest.

One human in the story, the hero, figured out he could identify the fallen angel–cannibal aliens by examining their naked backs. And the other thing about the incomers was this: They all had heterochromatic eyes.

I was trapped in that book and I couldn't get out.

:|:

So the entire story came to my father because a dead horse fell one hundred sideways miles and broke my back.

This is why I only take my shirt off around people who don't read—like Cade Hernandez and pretty much everybody associated with the Burnt Mill Creek High School Pioneers baseball team.

But Julia Bishop had been *looking* at my naked back that night, *examining me* as I lay facedown and practically naked in a puddle of piss on my living room floor. She *noticed* things. She'd seen my eyes. And anyone who'd read my father's novel would know right away that the scars on my back were exactly the same marks carried by the predatory incomers.

"When are we going to the party?" Monica asked. Her cellphone battery was dying, and she needed to get inside, to somewhere that had electrical outlets and objects moving faster than me and Julia.

Cade, supportive of his date, said, "Yeah. Let's go. Moons are boringer than shit."

So I stood and extended a hand to help Julia to her feet.

Our atoms touched.

It was electrifying, and I knew then that most of her and

most of me had come from exactly the same churning stew of nothingness all those billions of miles away from where we stood, under a perigee moon, at exactly that moment.

Twenty miles.

"Um. Look," I said to Julia, "Cade said he was sorry about not reading because my father is the guy who actually wrote that book. My last name is Easton. And my dad, Mike, writes as Easton Michaels."

Julia Bishop stared at me.

Her eyes widened, and the little moons got brighter.

"Really?" she said.

I nodded.

"Really," I confirmed.

Julia Bishop drove a brand-new Ford Mustang.

Cade complained about two things. The first being that Julia made him store his remaining beers inside the locked trunk.

Then he said, "This car's so small, if I get a raging hard-on back here, it's going to deploy your goddamned airbags."

"Nobody would want that," I said.

Monica Fassbinder giggled.

I offered an apologetic explanation to Julia Bishop. "Uh. Cade's kind of obsessed with his . . . uh. . . . Well, he's drunk. So, shut the hell up, Cade."

And Cade speculated, "What you would see if I held a mirror in back of my nutsack, Finner."

Then he poked a finger into my shoulder blade.

I rolled my eyes and sighed.

This was Cade Hernandez: set on a course of ruining everything.

Julia crawled her car across the creekbed and onto the highway.

"Do you think you could stop for a second at my house, just so I can be sure Laika made it home?"

"Okay," Julia said.

Cade whined, "We're never going to get there! I want another beer!"

"Five seconds, Cade."

One hundred sideways miles.

Cade was irritating me. It had been a tough night, but I didn't want it to end.

Not yet.

When we got to my house, Julia opened her door so she could follow me into the backyard. She left the motor running.

"I don't think that's a good idea," I said, eyeing Cade in the backseat. I felt certain he'd *borrow* that idling car of hers and drive off.

"Oh." Julia nodded.

She turned off the motor and took her keys.

Then we went through the yard and toward the back of the house to check on Laika.

Across the fence, I saw Mr. Castellan, the bullfighter, dumping garbage onto his incinerator. Incinerators are illegal in the canyon, but nobody seems to care enough to complain. Manny Castellan had atoms he needed to set free.

I pointed toward the glow of Mr. Castellan's fire and said to Julia, "My neighbor used to fight bulls in Mexico."

"Did he ever lose?" Julia asked.

I shrugged and shook my head. "I never asked him that."

Mr. Castellan didn't see us watching him. I noticed a while ago that Manuel Castellan walked like a bullfighter. He moved his legs like a gaited horse and held his chin just a bit higher than most men do.

A guy who moved like he did would never lose to a bull, I thought.

Sometimes his trash fires stunk pretty bad, depending on the types of atoms the bullfighter was freeing. This night, the smoke smelled of cinnamon and orange peel.

We went into the backyard.

"So your father actually made up *The Lazarus Door* just because of you?" Julia said.

"Yes."

"It must be cool to have a dad who's a famous writer, and to know that parts of you are in actual books," she said.

Books are the knackeries to what is real.

"Too many parts of me," I said.

I caught her glancing at me, smiling with her mouth closed.

"Sometimes it's like I've been trapped inside his book."

Julia said, "Oh."

"Besides, it's just the same as having a dad who does anything else," I said.

Laika's crate sat on the concrete deck between the patio and our pool. My dog lay curled up inside it, watching me.

Laika has a real issue with guilt.

I swung the little crate door shut and trapped her inside.

"Hah!" Julia said, "*Sputnik 2.*"

"Most people don't get it," I said.

"The space dog."

"The dog they killed."

"Maybe that's why she's attracted to dead things," Julia said.

I nodded. "You're probably right. You can't just name a dog Laika and then expect her to *not* be morbidly fascinated by decay. The name carries an awful lot of baggage."

"Space garbage."

Julia walked to the edge of the pool. I watched her. While the bullfighter walked like a gaited horse, Julia Bishop glided like a cat.

"This is a nice pool."

"I swim a lot. If baseball and swimming weren't at the same time, I'd probably be on swim. I'm pretty good. So's Cade. Maybe sometime you could, uh . . . come . . . swimming."

I didn't know that I honestly wanted her to. Just saying it made me feel flustered, worried, and more than a little turned on, thinking about how our unclothed bodies might actually be connected by all those sticky molecules of warm pool water.

:|:

"Let me see your back again," Julia said.

"No. I don't want to."

"Oh, come on. I think it's the coolest thing ever, and I already saw it anyway." She said, "I loved that book. Meeting you is like a miracle."

I shook my head.

Julia went on. "What would you say if I told you I took a picture of your Lazarus Door mark with my phone while you were lying on the floor?"

My face went straight.

"I would say that's probably the meanest thing anyone's ever done to me."

Julia pulled her phone from the back pocket of her shorts and handed it to me. It was warm.

She said, "You can look at my pictures. I didn't do it. I was only messing with you, Finn."

I gave Julia back her phone, turned around, and looked at the moon as I pulled my tank top up over my shoulders so she could see it.

:|:

The Lazarus Door mark.

The little things in my father's novel were called Lazarus Doors because you actually had to die to come through them— one atom at a time.

There was even a song people in the book sang, and soon everyone all over the messed-up, invaded, and cannibalized planet began to hear the song constantly in their heads. At first, some people thought they were receiving messages, that the song itself was the Voice of God.

The song went like this:

When the little door opens,
A tiny man crawls through.
He climbs down a ladder
And gets inside you.
One atom at a time,
One atom at a time.

:|:

"Well, what if you really *did* come through a Lazarus Door but you just don't remember doing it?" Julia said.

"Um. Sure." I sighed. "It's a novel. Novels are fiction. Some people got really crazy over that dumb book."

I pulled my shirt down and turned to face her.

"What happened to you, then?" Julia asked.

I suddenly stopped thinking about anything that I used to keep protected.

Things started to be freed, and the prison gates swung open.

Something was being rendered out of my heart in the knackery of this night.

I said, "A dead horse fell out of the sky and landed on me. It broke my back. It's why I blank out, have seizures. Cade calls it 'doing my thing.' That's the truth—that's what really happened, okay?"

"A dead horse?"

"Yes."

I looked directly into her eyes. "It fell out of a truck that was hauling it to a knackery—a rendering plant—where they turn dead things into all kinds of shit you never thought contained dead things."

"Well, I think whatever it is looks amazing. Like you actually came from another world. And you had no idea I was sitting there, trying to get you to say something?"

"No."

"That must be cool," Julia decided.

"I guess it is."

I shrugged.

"I wonder what it must be like."

"It's like emptying everything out of your head, but you can still see and hear and feel. And you don't care at all about who you are, or about anything, actually. It's, um, beautiful."

A car horn honked from the front of my house.

Cade Hernandez yelled, "Come! On! Fucker!"

I took a deep breath.

I said, "What? It's been, like, fifteen seconds."

Then Julia said, "I bet your girlfriend would be jealous if she knew I was driving you around, that I asked you to take off your shirt for me."

"Oh, sure."

"What's that supposed to mean?"

"You're messing with me again."

"I promise I'm not."

Twenty miles.

Twenty miles.

"Okay. Like I'd ever have a girlfriend," I said.

"Why?" Julia laughed. "Are you gay or something?"

She was beautifully exasperating.

I turned away from her and walked toward the front yard.

I said, "No."

Julia followed after me.

"Hey, wait. I'm sorry, Finn. I didn't mean to hurt your feelings."

"I'm fine, Julia."

:|:

She grabbed my hand as I rounded the corner, heading toward her car. Cade was in the front seat of Julia's Mustang, fumbling around to find the trunk release, no doubt to get to his locked-up beer.

I stopped, and Julia Bishop kissed me on the lips.

I smelled flowers. It was only her hair.

It was a short kiss, and to be honest my first reaction was to pull away from her. I had never kissed anyone on the mouth before. It startled and amazed me. Maybe that *did* make me gay or something. But my atoms were so confused. I felt like I could vaporize on the spot.

"What was that about?" I said.

"I'm sorry you're having such a sucky night, Finn."

"Nights like this come around only once every sixty billion miles," I said.

And it wasn't so bad after all.

BLAKE GRUNWALD'S SHITTY PARTY

"I'm not feeling so good," Cade said.

I wouldn't have expected anything to the contrary. Cade Hernandez had finished off at least ten beers that night, and as soon as we got to Blake Grunwald's ridiculously bad party, he started drinking gin, too.

Cade's skin, which was unblemished and usually glowed a radiant, healthy pink-peach, looked like slowly boiled pork fat.

I had a feeling there was a simmering stew of atoms inside Cade Hernandez's digestive tract that needed to be freed.

And as it later turned out, I was correct.

"I'm going to go find somewhere to lay down," Cade said.

"Maybe we should just leave," I offered.

"I don't think I should ride in Julia's car, dude."

Cade stood up, wobbling like a tightrope walker in a hurricane.

We had been sitting on a couch in Blake Grunwald's parents' living room—Cade, Monica, me, and Julia. The party was terrible. In the living room, about half of the baseball team were taking drunken turns at playing an NFL video game on Blake's parents' wide-screen television. A few girls were in there too, but most of them looked to be in junior high school, so between football plays the boys kept leering at Monica and Julia, and fidgeting conspicuously with their penises.

Most of the party took place outside, in Blake's parents' backyard, where scores of boys from Burnt Mill Creek gathered around gleaming kegs of beer, whooping and hollering over the dumbest and most inane masculine challenges, touching each other—which is something drunk boys at parties tend to do a bit too much—and smoking lots and lots of marijuana.

And every last boy at the party, even the seventh- and eighth-graders, somehow managed to stroll past our place on the couch, raise an eyebrow, and say the exact same thing, which was this: "Hey, Monica."

Monica Fassbinder's ambidextrous generosity was legendary in Burnt Mill Creek, but as far as I knew, it began and ended at Cade Hernandez.

"I better help you, dude."

I got up and put my arm around Cade's shoulders.

Blake Grunwald's parents' home was what real estate agents in California called seventies ranch style—which meant it was long and narrow, dark on the interior, and built on one level. I led Cade down a hallway behind the living room, assuming we'd find someplace where a boy could pass out and not be noticed.

It wouldn't be too much of a challenge, I thought. After seeing the mix of kids who'd come out to Blake Grunwald's crappy party, I was confident this would be a no-sex event.

Across from a bathroom done entirely in the same shade of pale green you'd expect to see inside the examining room at a fertility clinic, the last doorway in the hall opened onto a darkened bedroom. I didn't even need to turn on the light to know this was Blake's room.

Catchers' gear emits a particular damp-crotch boy smell. In the case of Blake Grunwald's catchers' gear, the scent produced a counteracting effect to how fertile I felt after glancing into the pastel green bathroom across the hall.

"Here," I said. "Lie down on Blake's bed. There's a bathroom just outside the door."

"Okay."

I deposited Cade Hernandez onto our backup catcher's nicely made bed. I picked up Cade's legs and put them on top of Blake's bedspread.

"Do you want some water or anything?" I asked.

"No. I'll be okay in a few minutes. Thanks, dude."

"Do you want me to take off your shoes?"

"Why the fuck are you wearing my shoes?"

"Uh . . ."

I pulled Cade's shoes from his feet. He was burning hot. I could feel the soggy heat rising from his body like he was a wet tea bag that had just been lifted from boiling water. So I pulled his damp socks off, tucked them into his shoes, which I placed on the floor at the foot of Blake's bed, and shut the door very quietly.

When I got back to the couch in Blake Grunwald's parents' living room, Monica Fassbinder and Julia Bishop were gone.

I realized too that Blake Grunwald had just come inside the house from his parents' backyard and stood glaring at me with his flabby chest puffed out and his arms bent back like a gun-slinger in an old Western.

This was definitely not a good time or place for me and Blake to rekindle our fistfight.

So I attempted to defuse the situation with a sober and sincere-sounding lie.

"Hey, Blake. Great party, man."

"Who told you you you could come and be here, Easton?"

Blake Grunwald was exceedingly drunk, stoned, chewing tobacco, and hurling an excess of pronouns too.

"Oh, uh, Cade said it it it was okay as long as we brought some girls."

"What girls?" Blake demanded.

"Uh. They were here just a minute ago," I said. "Maybe they're outside. Getting high. Smoking the weed. Man."

I only hoped that Julia wasn't like that. I had the idea she wasn't, but it's always so hard to tell these things about kids.

Blake said, "Huh?" and glanced over his shoulder, out the sliding, postmodern seventies-style glass door through which he'd entered. And as soon as he did, I spun around and headed for the front exit.

Monica Fassbinder and Julia Bishop stood on the curb beside Julia's Mustang. Monica smoked a cigarette, taking big, dramatic, disaffected drags.

"You guys can't take off," I said. "Blake Grunwald wants to *kill me*."

"Why does he want to do that?" Julia asked.

Monica Fassbinder, being a sort of mascot to Cade Hernandez, knew all about our issues.

"We just hate each other," I said.

"Oh," Julia said with a tone that implied she understood perfectly well that sometimes boys just hated each other for insignificant reasons.

"Well, Monica asked if I would take her home," she said. "I was going to come back to get you."

"You can't leave me here," I said. "I'll ride with you."

I realized this meant I would be the solitary boy riding with Monica Fassbinder and Julia Bishop inside a brand-new Ford Mustang, and it made my atoms feel very fertile.

Monica exhaled a cloud of cigarette smoke and said, "What about Cade?"

"Uh, he needs to sleep for a while. He'll be okay. Julia and I will come back for him. We'll keep him safe for you, Monica."

So that's how I ended up alone with Julia Bishop, driving twenty miles per second through the deserted streets of Burnt Mill Creek after midnight, and under the second brightest moon in more than a century.

Sixty billion miles.

"What about you?" I said. "Won't your boyfriend want to kick my ass for getting you to drive me and my wasted friends to a shitty party?"

We'd dropped Monica Fassbinder off at her host family's house, which happened to be across the street from the left-field fence at Burnt Mill Creek High School's baseball diamond. Monica's host "mother," Mrs. Shoemaker, was a substitute teacher at our school.

I'll admit my question was a rather obvious way of asking

what I didn't have the nerve to say directly to Julia Bishop.

She said, "Finn Easton, Right Field."

"How did you know what position I play?"

Julia kept her eyes fixed forward. We stopped at a red light on Old Mill Boulevard, at an intersection across from Flat Face Pizza.

"Because I'm a stalker and I ruin boys' lives," Julia said blankly.

"Oh."

Then she laughed.

"I'm in the yearbook class. I looked you up," she said.

I remembered seeing "Yearbook" on her class schedule the day I showed her around the school, and I wondered if she'd been as interested in finding out about me as I was about her.

That couldn't possibly be the case, I thought.

"Oh," I said. To be honest, I was relieved that she was only messing with me and that she wasn't actually a stalker who ruined boys' lives.

Then she said, "I wasn't stalking you or anything. It's just that I didn't know anyone here at all. You were the first nonadult person I met, so I remembered your name. And I looked at your pictures."

"Oh," I repeated.

"You say that a lot."

"Uh."

"But my boyfriend wouldn't kick your ass, anyway. He's in Illinois."

"That would be a long way to come just to kick someone's ass," I said.

I knew I was stupid for feeling it, but when Julia Bishop

ANDREW SMITH

admitted she had a boyfriend, I kind of sank lower in my seat and thought about what a loser I was.

"It wouldn't be too long for him," Julia said. "He's an airline pilot."

"Oh."

Somehow, I didn't think it was overly strange for Julia Bishop to have a boyfriend who was probably in his forties, even if it was really creepy. My throat knotted up when I thought about how, if Julia Bishop's boyfriend actually was an airline pilot in his forties, then they most likely had sex all the time.

That's what forty-year-old airline pilots are going to do, after all: have sex. What other things could possibly happen between them? Conversations about prevailing headwinds or what happened today in high school yearbook fucking class?

I worked myself up into an angry storm rather quickly; another Finn Easton patented wild mood swing.

Then Julia laughed. "I'm just messing with you."

"Uh, I knew that," I said, but I didn't really.

"Would you smile?" Julia asked.

"I *am* smiling," I said.

"No, you're not."

"This is how I smile," I said. "I smile with my atoms on the inside."

"Try getting some of the outside ones to show it."

"I can't."

:|:

Julia Bishop moved to San Francisquito Canyon, which is the site of the worst human-caused engineering disaster in California history, from Chicago, which is the site of one of the tallest buildings in the United States.

Somebody in Illinois must have studied engineering at a regular school.

Imagine that.

Julia Bishop was nothing if not mysterious.

She told me very little about her life, and why she'd come to move two thousand miles during the last months of her eleventh-grade year.

Julia Bishop was beautiful and evasive.

"The earth moves two thousand miles, the distance from Chicago to Burnt Mill Creek, in one minute and forty seconds," I said.

"It only took my parents about that long to decide to send me away from home," Julia Bishop said.

"I wish you'd quit doing that—messing with me," I said.

"I'm not," Julia said. "I'm really not messing with you. I needed to get away from there for a while, so they moved me out here to live with my aunt and uncle."

"So. Um. Why did you need to get away?" I asked.

"It doesn't matter anymore. And I kind of don't want to talk about it."

I felt my face redden. I suppose I got somewhat angry at her game playing. Julia Bishop had seen my most embarrassing and hidden truths, and I knew almost nothing about her. I turned my face and looked out the passenger-side window.

"It's going to be a left turn up there," I said.

"Are you mad or something?"

"No."

"You *sound* mad," she said.

"This is how my atoms sound when I'm happy," I answered.

"You're full of shit, Finn Easton."

Julia let the car drift slowly toward the curb. We were on the street where Blake Grunwald lived, but the house was halfway down the block.

Julia Bishop parked there.

She said, "I don't really like to say what happened. Is that okay?"

"It's your story," I said. "It's okay for you to tell it or not tell it."

"Okay," she said.

"Okay," I agreed.

Julia stared down the street as though she were looking to see who was still hanging out in front of Blake Grunwald's shitty party, but I could tell she was really trying to figure out how to talk to me, how to *crack* me.

She said, "I *did* have a boyfriend there."

"Oh."

"It's not like that," Julia said. "Well, it kind of got out of control with him and he started doing things that scared me, scared the shit out of my parents."

"Like, was he dangerous?" I asked.

"Totally."

"Do you want me to go to Chicago and kick his ass?" I asked.

Julia smiled and shook her head.

"So, then—just checking—he doesn't really fly airplanes, does he?"

"No. He played on my school's hockey team."

I calculated probabilities. "Oh. Baseball players generally don't fare so well in matchups against hockey players."

Julia laughed.

She said, "You never even kissed a girl before, did you?"

"Where did *that* come from?" I asked.

Julia nodded up at the sky. "Out there."

"Is it so obvious?"

"Yes."

"Well, you're right. I haven't ever kissed a girl. Um. Before. . . ."

"It's all behind you now."

I thought about how long ago it had been—since Julia Bishop grabbed my arm, spun me around, and kissed me.

"It was about a hundred thousand miles, I guess, since the last time I kissed a girl."

"I like how you do that."

I didn't know what she could possibly be talking about. She certainly couldn't have been referring to my abilities as a kisser.

"You like how I do *what*?" I said.

"The way you think about how far we go in space. I never thought about that stuff at all before I talked to you tonight. To me, it all just seems empty and nowhere—like we never really get anywhere at all. I mean, when you—when most people—look up there, nobody ever really thinks those are actual places that we're moving toward. You make everything seem so big, like it really matters. I think it's something remarkable that you made me think about how far we actually move."

I shifted in my seat. I was unbearably hot; I needed some air.

"I can't help it. It's what I do. Kind of like you messing with me is what you do."

"I'm not messing with you, Finn. I really think you're an okay guy."

"Oh. Okay."

When Julia Bishop said I was an "okay guy," my atoms began to swirl and vibrate. I felt very aroused and daring.

I said, "Tell me something. It's hard for me to figure out if I'm normal and shit with a best friend like Cade Hernandez. And I don't know anything about kids in Chicago, or hockey players, or girls who look like you. So. Did you and your old boyfriend—you know, did you guys have sex?"

Julia laughed. "Where'd *that* come from?"

"A Lazarus Door," I said.

Julia said, "Oh. Well. You know what? We shouldn't have."

I said, "Oh. Um. Sorry. I shouldn't have asked you that."

"It's okay."

I wasn't looking at her when I apologized for asking my question. I was too flustered to because all I could think about at that exact moment was Julia Bishop having sex with some hockey-playing beast from Chicago, and what it would be like if she ever had sex with me.

She put her hand on mine, and I swallowed the knot in my throat.

Twenty miles.

Twenty miles.

Then I leaned across the gearshift and kissed Julia Bishop.

Inside the swirling calamity of our kiss, as we parted our lips and explored each other's tongues, I turned completely inside out.

I poured myself into Julia Bishop's warm, delicious mouth. We sailed along, wrapped wholly and firmly together, flying twenty miles, twenty miles, twenty miles, twenty miles. And in that turning, unfolding, opening, I forgot everything about me. It was as if all the words anyone ever dreamed up migrated from my head, through my mouth, and into Julia Bishop, a flooding exodus of everything uncontained, all those nouns, articles, verbs, emptying me completely.

Our kiss lasted only about one hundred sideways miles, but it was the best stretch of distance my fourteen-billion-year-old sexually inflamed teenage atoms had ever covered.

Julia slid her hand up inside my tank top. She rubbed my chest and pinched at my nipples.

It was wild.

I desperately wished to make everything else just stop, so Julia Bishop and I could stay there, wrapped up in each other forever—so we could let everything else on this world slide endlessly past us into the big black knackery of our universe.

I jumped when something slapped against my window.

Cade Hernandez.

He said, "Dudes, you're giving me a total boner."

That made two of us.

Cade Hernandez looked as though he'd recovered, at least, but he was missing a few articles of clothing. In fact, all he had on were the blue jeans he'd worn earlier when he went to work at Flat Face Pizza. And his fly was half-open. You could see the white of his underwear.

Cade Hernandez was a mess.

Cade stood on the curb barefoot, sockless, and naked from the waist up.

I opened the car door and attempted to stand. I grabbed myself with both hands and pulled my tank top down to cover the embarrassing bulge inside my flimsy shorts.

"Um," I said, "where's the rest of you?"

"Oh, don't worry about it." Cade flipped the seat forward and climbed into the back of the Mustang.

"We need to go back to Blake's to get Cade's clothes," I told Julia.

"Did you guys leave Monica there?" Cade asked.

"I drove her home," Julia said.

"Then you should just take me and Finner back to his house," Cade said. "I don't think it would be a good idea to go back to Blake's house for my shit."

I said, "Um."

Cade continued. "When I woke up, I couldn't figure out where I was and shit. All I knew was it smelled like a fucking sweaty locker room. It smelled like Blake's balls. And then I just started puking everywhere. All over Blake's fucking bed."

I found this to be very funny.

Who wouldn't laugh at a guy like Cade Hernandez vomiting in the bed of an asshole like Blake Grunwald?

Cade said, "It was bad, dude. Really. I must have puked a gallon all over his pillows and sheets. I tried to get up, but I just kept puking and puking. Then I finally made it into the hall, and I puked all over the floor there, too."

"Those carpets were nice," I said.

"Berber," Cade affirmed.

He went on. "I tried to make it to the bathroom, and I kept puking and puking all over everything—the door, the wall, the counters, the linen rack. By the time I made it to the toilet, I was pretty much emptied out. But I did puke in the bathtub and on the toilet lid too."

"What happened to your shirt?" I asked.

Cade shook his head. "I left it under Blake's pillow. It was fucking destroyed, dude. I have no idea what happened to my shoes and socks."

"Um."

I heard Cade flipping his can of chewing tobacco.

He announced in a very cheerful voice, "I do feel a hell of a lot better now, though."

"Nothing like a good puke to make you feel alive again," I said.

Cade packed a wad of tobacco into his lower lip and added, "But I don't think I should go back for my clothes and shit. Blake's gonna be fucking pissed."

"Yeah," I agreed, "that's probably not such a good idea."

Sometimes kids just have to write off lost articles of clothing at the end of a party.

THE GOVERNOR OF CALIFORNIA

Julia Bishop dropped Cade Hernandez and me off at my house at three o'clock in the morning.

I gave her my phone number.

I wanted so desperately to kiss her again, just like we did when Julia parked her car on Blake Grunwald's street. But I was afraid to do something as bold as that with Cade watching.

What an idiot I was.

It was very frustrating for me—being torn between the need to taste Julia Bishop in my mouth one more time and my unwillingness to risk failure in front of my sexually accomplished best friend.

Now there's a guaranteed formula for extinction.

Cade Hernandez and I did not wake up until noon. When we got out of bed, Cade, moaning, walked downstairs and let himself out into the backyard. He stood at the edge of our pool, held his arms out like airplane wings, and then, wearing nothing at all but white cotton briefs, let himself fall into the cool water.

"Don't pee in my pool, Cade," I warned.

"Dude, I always pee in your pool. Why should today be any different?"

Laika whimpered inside *Sputnik 2*.

I let her out with a warning. "And stay away from me. You stink."

My dog slunk away to a shaded corner of the backyard. I was neither physically nor mentally prepared to deal with bathing the wretched odor of dead coyote atoms from Laika's oily fur so early in the teenage day.

Cade assumed a faceup dead-man's float in the middle of the pool.

He said, "I am so fucking hungover, dude."

Here was my friend, floating in his underwear in my pool.

I said, "You'd never know it, Cade."

Cade added, "Be a pal and toss my can of chew out here. I can't move."

"Uh."

Maybe it was our late bedtime, or perhaps the lingering after-effects of my blanking out the day before, or the sleepless sweaty night I spent fantasizing about having sex with Julia Bishop, but something struck me as being eerily still and quiet that day. It was as though things had changed, that somehow the earth had frozen in its journey and time had finally come to a standstill.

That would be nice.

I thought, even on a Sunday morning there would be plenty of traffic noise through the canyon—obese weekend Harley riders traveling in packs up to the old bikers' bar called the Rock Inn, airplanes flying overhead, the ambient weekend sounds of Southern California in its constant buzz and rumble.

But that morning, everything was still.

Cade couldn't have noticed. He only floated there in his briefs with his eyes shut, grinning peacefully. He might as well have been a billion miles away with his hangover.

I tossed the tin of tobacco out to Cade. He packed some into his lower lip and flipped the can over to the deck at the edge of the deep end.

I went back inside the house and slipped into some trunks.

When we pulled into the student lot at Burnt Mill Creek High School on Monday morning, the campus had been made over, decorated with California flags and colorful banners. Along the chain-link fence that separated the parking lot from the school stretched an enormous painted sign:

WELCOME TO BURNT MILL CREEK HIGH
SCHOOL, GOVERNOR ALTVATTER!

The first bell rang. We hurried through the gate so we wouldn't be late to Mr. Nossik's class and fan the flames of hatred for all things Cade Hernandez so early in our week of freedom.

"What do you think *that's* all about?" Cade said.

"I don't know. A friendly reminder, I guess."

I pointed at the welcome banner. Beneath Governor Altvatter's name, someone—a foot soldier in Cade's Stop Trying to Make Us Stop revolution—had scrawled in black permanent marker:

AND DON'T FORGET TO NOT SAY "FUCK"! THANK YOU!

Cade nodded in agreement. "It's the polite thing to do, after all."

For some reason, Burnt Mill Creek had an inordinately large population of Germans—families with last names such as Schwarzkopf, Grunwald, or Shoemaker. The first German residents of this town with no creek and no mill actually settled here during World War I, when Hate the Hun campaigns were heating up in other, more populated regions of America.

And our school always seemed to attract German exchange students, and teachers who enjoyed dressing up as Nazis.

Mr. Nossik was from Canada.

Burnt Mill Creek High School even had a traditional all-boys German Dance Club. They were the most unpopular kids on campus. Although the students of Burnt Mill Creek had largely abandoned what at one time had been considered boys-being-boys typical teenage bullying, the German Dance Club was still fair game.

Look: Who doesn't feel compelled to rough up a knee-slapping kid who's wearing lederhosen and a Tyrolean hat?

Anyway, Blake Grunwald was in the German Dance Club.

And Governor Altvatter was German too.

So we didn't really know what was going on with all the flags and the special visit and so on, but as soon as we got to first period history, Mr. Nossik escorted us to the gym, where the entire eleventh-grade class had gathered in order to hear a special message just for us from Governor Altvatter.

The assembly began with our cherubic lederhosen-and-Tyrolean-hat-wearing German Dance Club boys stomping their feet and slapping their naked pink knees.

It was ridiculous.

Such assemblies were just about the only place the German Dance Club could safely perform and *not* get beaten up, so the junior class sat through a spectacle that was most likely intended to be endured only by an audience at least fifteen beers into the night. And it was a good thing that the Hofbräuhaus music accompanying the boys was so loud, because more than a few of the kids in the bleachers fired off barrages of F-bombs.

In fact, at the conclusion of the dance, while nobody at all was clapping, our principal—Mr. Baumgartner—who was dressed in a fuck shirt, introduced Governor Altvatter, who was also wearing a fuck shirt, although it was put on over the stiff-collar-and-tie uniform mandated by the state's highest political office.

There were press photographers in the gym too, and even a camera crew from our local *Eye on Burnt Mill Creek* news program, which broadcast on a cable channel absolutely no one ever subscribed to. And although the gym was eerily quiet (there were only about two hundred of us kids, after all), when he approached the speaker's podium, Governor Altvatter raised his arms in the standardized politician's gesture aimed at focusing a wildly enthusiastic crowd on the magnificence of his monstrous ego.

"What a douche bag," Cade Hernandez whispered.

Then Governor Altvatter said, "Hello, Burnt Mill Creek High School Pioneers!"

Naturally, we were expected to cheer or answer back or do something.

But nobody really knew what to say, since we were all sixteen- or seventeen-year-old kids who didn't give a shit about our governor and had not been prepped on delivering a coordinated choral response.

So there was only chaotic noise.

I heard Cade Hernandez say, "Hello, Governor Oldfucker!"

Which, I believe, is more or less what Altvatter means, translated from the German.

Enough kids around Cade heard it too. This was the group that started clapping and chanting "Oldfucker! Oldfucker! Oldfucker! Oldfucker!"

Given the bad acoustics of the gym, it was impossible to be certain the Burnt Mill Creek High School Pioneers weren't actually chanting *Altvatter! Altvatter! Altvatter! Altvatter!* So the governor, beaming, raised his hands again and stared down at his notes on the podium with a look of practiced, aw-shucks humility on his face.

"Thank you. Thank you," the governor began. Then he cleared his throat and looked seriously at our innocent little faces and said, "Principal Baumgartner knows the reason for my visit to you—the eleventh-grade class here at Burnt Mill Creek High School. I have come here today to say *job well done* and *congratulations*, for being the history-making class in which every last one of you scored a rating of Advanced on last year's California BEST Test. It is truly a testament to the leadership you fine young men and women have here at Burnt Mill Creek!"

"Holy fuck!" someone sitting behind Cade Hernandez whispered.

"We're fucking geniuses," another kid said.

And later that day, delivery trucks arrived at Burnt Mill Creek High School. The governor of the state of California bought every single eleventh-grade Pioneer ice cream sandwiches. Workers from the trucks gave each one of us colorful bags that

ANDREW SMITH

said VISIT SACRAMENTO! and we walked through rows of tables, filling our Sacramento Tourism bags with toothpaste and soap and toothbrushes and packages of brand-new underwear.

The underwear and stuff came from a disaster-relief warehouse that had to be shut down because of the state budget cuts.

Cade Hernandez was a god.

PART 2

THE PERSEIDS

UNLUCKY LINDY

Think about how fast twenty miles per second is: It is so fast that every last thing on the planet of humans and dogs is, in essence, traveling at just about the same absolute speed—whether you're talking about a jet aircraft in flight, a dead horse falling from the sky, or the entire state of Oklahoma at rest.

It's all pretty much the same.

About one week, twelve million miles, after my family returned home from New York City, our history teacher, Mr. Nossik, dressed up as the famed aviator Charles Lindbergh.

Dead history came to life once again at Burnt Mill Creek High School.

Cade Hernandez was in one of those perfectly energized Cade Hernandez moods, too, which meant there would be war. I knew it immediately, and Cade was well armed.

As soon as we walked into Mr. Nossik's classroom together, I sensed how Cade paused and stiffened up just a little at seeing how our history teacher was dressed.

Things could have been so much easier for Mr. Nossik if Cade Hernandez and I had history class later in the day. Cade was always so much more sedate and less agitated after his rendezvous with Monica Fassbinder in the night-custodian's shed, which usually happened just before lunch.

Unfortunately, we had American history with Mr. Nossik first thing in the morning, when Cade Hernandez could always be counted on to be all fired up and freshly buzzed on nicotine.

That day, Mr. Nossik wore a leather aviator's helmet. It made him look like a bloated turtle. Around his neck dangled a pair of goggles, and he also had on a tightly buttoned brown leather jacket, knickers that fanned out at his thighs, and black kneesocks.

Nobody would have known who Mr. Nossik was supposed to be. For all we kids knew or cared, he could have been a serial killer, because the way he was dressed looked exceedingly creepy. But he had prepared us by writing block letters on the board that said the following:

CHARLES LINDBERGH'S FLIGHT—MAY 21, 1927

It also happened to be May twenty-first that day.

When we sat down, I whispered to Cade, "Go easy on him. He doesn't look right. I think that helmet thing might be stopping the blood in his head."

It was like asking a cat not to kill a bird.

Well, to be accurate, cats enjoy playing with birds before killing them.

Cade just stared and stared at Mr. Nossik.

Cade Hernandez shook his head.

He whispered back to me, "That thing on his head makes him look like a five-foot-long condom."

Mr. Nossik was not very tall.

Cade smiled and kept his unblinking eyes focused on our teacher. It was a look that was particular to Cade Hernandez—a seducer's look. It was magical and unavoidable and caused women to willingly enslave themselves to him. And I'll admit it—sometimes when Cade Hernandez looked at me with that particular expression, I'd get flustered and embarrassed and have to turn away in frustration and sexual doubt.

But before anything at all could happen, Mr. Nossik scrunched his brows together and pointed directly at Cade Hernandez's chest.

"You!" he said over the top of his stiffened index finger. "I want *you* to go to the back of the room and turn around so I don't have to look at you. I just can't stand looking at your face right now."

And Cade wasn't doing a thing.

Well, except staring at Mr. Nossik with his seducer's eyes.

"I'm not doing anything, Mr. Nossik."

Cade's voice was as sweet as jasmine flowers on an early summer evening.

"I can tell you're about to say something to me."

Mr. Nossik was already sweating.

"I'm not going to say anything, Mr. Nossik. I promise."

I was certain the music of Cade's plea and the look in his eyes at that moment caused several girls in the classroom to spontaneously ovulate.

"Go to the back or I will throw you out of my room, Mr. Hernandez!"

This was a regular occurrence in Mr. Nossik's classroom. The old tight-buttoned fool never realized he was only making Cade out to be a bigger, more martyred hero in the hearts of his classmates.

So Cade Hernandez, with sorrow-widened blue eyes, quietly stood and went back to the "Cade Desk," which had been permanently turned away from the front of the room.

One time I asked Cade if it hurt his feelings when Mr. Nossik singled him out and sent him away for no apparent reason. Cade was dead serious when he told me *yes*. I felt bad for him. For all his button-pushing prowess, Cade Hernandez was honestly sad about the way Mr. Nossik treated him at times, and I couldn't blame him for it.

So Mr. Nossik started in with his lecture about the accomplishments and difficult life of Charles Lindbergh. To be honest, nobody paid much attention. I think most of the kids in the class were waiting to see what Cade Hernandez was going to do to get Lucky Lindy to crash and burn.

We all thought Cade would go right to work, too, because almost as soon as Mr. Nossik began telling about Lindbergh's life before the historic transatlantic crossing, Cade shot his hand up in the air, rigid, straight, and sincere, with that earnest Cade Hernandez look on his face as he stared and stared over his shoulder into Mr. Nossik's softening eyes.

What could he possibly do?

Nobody else in the entire class had a hand raised.

Mr. Nossik ultimately broke down and called on Cade.

He sighed, exasperated. "What is it, Mr. Hernandez?"

And Cade, in the loveliest voice imaginable, said this: "Mr.

Nossik, I read that Charles Lindbergh was more than a little racist, that he was obsessed with white supremacy—as though he believed the most urgent priority for us during the Second World War was not to defeat totalitarianism but to preserve the white race. Was that really *true*?"

Mr. Nossik looked very confused. Here was Cade Hernandez, in exile at the back of the classroom, asking a perfectly reasonable question about a figure from history. Cade, as I have said before, was actually a very smart kid.

He was also a cat that had just so gently set his claws into Lucky Lindy's plumage.

Mr. Nossik said, "Um . . ."

And Cade sank his claws deeper.

"How long did it take Charles Lindbergh to fly to Paris?"

Mr. Nossik's left eye twitched just a little. I noticed it. He had to have been thinking a bomb was about to drop, that Cade Hernandez was about to deploy a heat-seeking missile. If he was thinking that, he would have been correct.

Mr. Nossik answered, "About thirty-four hours."

Cade said, "Thirty-four hours is a really long time. Do you suppose Charles Lindbergh masturbated at least once or twice during that flight, Mr. Nossik?"

The bird was a goner.

The kids in the class laughed.

Mr. Nossik's face began to swell within the confines of his leather turtle cap.

"Cade, go stand outside!" he said.

And Cade said, "I know I would have masturbated *at least* once or twice if I was all alone in an airplane for thirty-four hours. And, Mr. Nossik, did you know NASA *told* the astronauts on the *Skylab* mission in the 1970s that they were *required* to masturbate up there in space, every day, just to stay healthy? Imagine that—a government agency actually *ordering* a guy to masturbate. What's wrong with *this* picture? What guy honestly needs to be *ordered* to masturbate? Astronauts, and maybe Charles Lindbergh, need to be told, I guess."

"Get! Out!" Mr. Nossik demanded.

"Well, it *is* true about *Skylab*," Cade said. He went on, and I could almost hear the little bird bones crunching in the toothy jaws of the cat. "And I saw how Charles Lindbergh had made himself a special little tube to pee in from his pilot's seat. Did you know that? It was really small, too. I don't think there's any way a normal guy's penis would ever fit into that thing."

Cade Hernandez raised his right hand in front of his chin, nodding confidently and gapping his thumb and index finger about three-fourths of an inch.

You have to admit: That's small enough to believe your family line is cursed.

Our teacher fumbled urgently with the neck fasteners on his aviator helmet. He moved like he was on fire and his head was about to pop. Mr. Nossik went over to his chair and sat heavily.

Then Mr. Nossik turned red and slumped across his desk.

Mr. Nossik died the next day from a brain aneurysm.

That's the absolute truth.

Mr. Nossik reentered the great knackery of the universe. His atoms decided they could not bear holding on to one another as long as Cade Hernandez's atoms were determined to do likewise.

The kids in our history class at Burnt Mill Creek High School all believed Cade was some sort of superhero who could inflict brain aneurysms at will. Of course this was not the case. Still, nobody ever messed with Cade Hernandez after that, not even Blake Grunwald, our German-dancer backup catcher who had a definite score to settle with my friend.

Who wants an aneurysm?

Cade Hernandez never felt guilty or strange about the death of Mr. Nossik. Although it was easy enough to consider Mr. Nossik's aneurysm a fateful coincidence, it was also a certainty that Cade Hernandez would have eventually pushed that old man so far that our history teacher would have ended up bringing a gun to school and shooting one of the state's best left-handed pitchers. Nobody would have wanted to see that.

Cade Hernandez was the kind of kid you'd dedicate hundred-foot-high monuments to, just so he wouldn't kill you with his lethal powers of annoyance.

Good thing he was my best friend.

One time later that summer, I sincerely asked Cade to do me a favor and please not give my father an aneurysm.

I AM NOT A CANNIBAL

By July sixteenth, which was my birthday, I had fallen wildly in love with Julia Bishop.

After traveling nearly eleven billion miles in my lifetime, my atoms and I had arrived at a place where we could confidently make such determinations about love.

Love makes atoms sticky.

Sticky atoms want to hold on to one another.

To be truly accurate, I fell in love with Julia Bishop the night of Blake Grunwald's shitty party, but I was afraid to admit such a thing to myself. I was scared I would ruin it, that things would unravel in the most horrible ways, and that I would have to go on simply pretending—as always—to be *fine*.

:|:

I knew this about Julia Bishop: She was a miracle—artistic, imaginative, and gifted—and she also liked to mess with me.

• • •

The last day of June, some time after school had been out for summer break, Julia Bishop drove her Mustang up into San Francisquito Canyon. We both wanted to hike around the tumbled ruins of William Mulholland's St. Francis Dam. Like most people who lived in the canyon, I had driven past plenty of times but never actually visited the site of the disaster.

And I had never gone anywhere alone with anyone who was a teenager and was also *not* Cade Hernandez.

My atoms were all riled up, and especially sticky that day.

At a bend in the snaking canyon road, just past the spot where San Francisquito Creek makes a ten-foot waterfall during rainy seasons, the city of Los Angeles built an impressive Art Deco–style power-generating plant.

It was creatively named Power Plant No. 1.

As a practice, I prefer to avoid abbreviations and to write out numbers, as opposed to using numerals. It's one of my quirks, like calculating distances rather than time. But the plant was actually named as I have written—with the abbreviation and the numeral as well—like *Sputnik 2*.

Power Plant No. 1 was completely wiped out by a twelve-billion-gallon wall of water in 1928. Starting at the location of the dam, and continuing all the way along the Santa Clara River bed toward the Pacific Ocean, perhaps as many as one hundred electric-company employees lost their lives.

The power plant was easily replaced, although nobody knows for certain how many irreplaceable people had been swallowed up in William Mulholland's churning liquid knackery.

In 1928 a group of thirty or so Native American Indians had been living on one of the large ranches below the St. Francis Dam.

One month before the disaster, a medicine man hunting deer in the canyon claimed to have received a vision of the catastrophe that would befall the dam. The medicine man warned the other Indians to leave the area. The Indians left the area the day before the collapse of the dam.

Imagine that.

Ten years ago, during one of the wettest winters on record, a large portion of the canyon road was washed away by the flooding of the San Francisquito Creek. The ruined highway shut down for more than a year—over half a billion miles. When a new roadway was finally opened, a stretch of the old ruined blacktop next to the rebuilt Power Plant No. 1 became a sort of parking area for the very few people who, knowing anything at all about William Mulholland's historic failure, traveled up here to see firsthand what was left of the St. Francis Dam.

Look: Even right here in Southern California, most people had never heard of the St. Francis Dam. The majority of Southern Californians simply assumed William Mulholland must have been someone magnificent because he had such a nice road, which meandered through the wealthiest communities in Los Angeles, named for him.

People probably would have remembered the St. Francis Dam better if its collapsing failure had caused the cancelation of an Academy Awards presentation, as opposed to just killing about five hundred innocent victims.

Julia Bishop parked her Mustang off the highway, along the chain-link fence that surrounded Power Plant No. 1.

"Are you okay?" she said. "You've been really quiet all day."

"Um."

"You're not—you know—feeling *weird*, are you?"

"I'm okay."

:|:

Usually, whenever someone asked me if I felt like I was going to have a seizure, which I could tell was Julia's underlying question, it would make me angry. But not with Julia. She could ask me anything at all and I would tell her the truth.

And the truth was that I was nervous about being alone with Julia Bishop.

Up to that point, Julia and I had spent time together at each other's houses, but we'd never technically been on a *date*. In fact, the first catastrophic time we had been truly alone together, I was either lying facedown in a puddle of urine, blanked out on the floor of my living room, or standing on my upstairs landing, naked and wrapped in a bath towel with the pattern of a seafoam green nautilus shell coiled directly in front of my penis.

No wonder I was nervous.

And even though we'd kissed that first night outside Blake Grunwald's shitty party, I had been plagued by the thought that Julia Bishop had kissed me—and run her delicious and soothing hand up inside my shirt—only because she'd felt *sorry* for the poor epileptic kid who had never been kissed in all those miles of his life.

So I took a deep breath and said, "Is this a *date*, Julia? Because I . . . we've never actually been anywhere alone together on purpose, and, well, I . . ."

Julia laughed and shook her head.

"You think too much," she said.

"Uh."

Julia put her hand on my knee. My bare knee. I was wearing shorts.

My wardrobe choice was based more on the heat of the day than on the likelihood of sexual arousal. Bad planning.

I felt very sticky at that moment.

I wondered what it would be like to feel Julia Bishop's hand slip up inside my shorts.

And then I blurted out, "I'm a Jew."

That's when Julia Bishop started to laugh for real.

"What?" she said.

"A Jew. I am a Jew."

Julia laughed so hard, tears pooled at the corners of her eyes. I felt terrible—like I'd made her cry. And I wanted to kiss her so bad and tell her I was sorry.

I was such a calamitous whirlwind of stupidity!

So I explained to Julia about my *real* mother, and how, technically, it made me a Jew.

"I don't know why I felt I had to say that," I explained. "Sometimes I think I feel the need to clarify my origins. I'm not, like, a *real* Jew, but I am a Jew."

Julia wiped her eyes.

"That's the dumbest thing I ever heard."

"Oh. Uh. Sorry."

"Anyway, you still can't prove to me you actually *didn't* come through a Lazarus Door."

:|:

I phrased the following as a question: "I haven't eaten anyone?"

Julia laughed again.

In my father's science fiction book, the one that caused such a tremendous stir, all the aliens who'd come here through Lazarus Doors took the names of angels from the Bible and from the Koran.

It made it easier to lure Christians and Muslims onto the aliens' dinner plates, but it also upset a lot of contemporary readers here on the planet of humans and dogs.

You could imagine.

One of the characters also happened to be a boy named Finn. But it wasn't me, my father always swore. He only *named* the incomer boy after me. Writers do that all the time, my father said. Thankfully, in spite of my Lazarus Door marks and heterochromatic eyes, as far as I know there was never an angel named Finn in any religion.

Julia said, "Well, I'm half-black."

I knew that. Unlike the Jew thing, half-black was something I could see. I never *asked* Julia Bishop about it. What would I say, anyway?

Hey, are you half-black?

And what did it matter? I supposed that was what Julia Bishop laughed about—the thought of her walking up to me and asking, *Hey, Finn, by any chance are you a Jew?*

Besides all that, Julia's aunt and uncle—the people she lived with across the canyon—were black.

There was no question of that.

So I said, "Um. I kind of knew that."

"Just wanted to clarify my origins," Julia said. "My mother is a black woman. My father owns a restaurant. I have never eaten anyone either. Can I tell you something?"

She still had her hand on my knee. It felt wonderfully terrifying.

I said, "If it's about my legs, I don't shave them. That's just how they are."

Julia laughed.

"It's not about you shaving your legs."

"Is it about food?"

I was so nervous, it felt like my heart was playing xylophone against my rib cage.

"No. It's about why I came here. The real reason."

Outside of that first awkward attempt on the night of the perigee moon to discover Julia Bishop's past, we had never really talked about the reason behind her relocation to California.

"Only if you want to," I said.

Julia stared directly into the eye of her steering wheel.

"Charlie—that's the guy I used to go out with back home—he raped me. That's why my parents wanted me to get away from the old school. All the kids, you know?"

Every atom of air fled from my lungs.

What can you say when someone you're in love with tells you something like that?

I mean, it's easy enough to laugh when you put your hand on a guy's bare knee and he stupidly blurts out, "I'm a Jew! I don't shave my legs!" because he's so confused, he doesn't know what else to say, but what can you say to something like *that*?

Twenty miles.

Twenty miles.

Twenty miles.

I turned away from her and stared out the side window. It wasn't fair. Nothing ever is.

"Are you okay?" I whispered.

:||:

"I'll be okay," Julia said.

Twenty miles.

And Julia said, "I'm sorry if it bothers you. I mean me telling you and all. You're the first *real* person I ever told."

"Sometimes I'm not sure I am a real person, Julia."

Julia smiled with her lips closed and shook her head.

"If I could push the world back all those miles with my bare hands and make it change direction, I would do that, Julia."

"Then I would never have gone out walking in the moonlight and found you."

"That's okay," I said. "I'm really sorry."

:||:

Julia patted my leg.

She leaned over and kissed me on the side of my head.

I felt terrible.

She said, "Let's go see that stupid dam."

"Watch out for ghosts."

"Ghosts are terrified of Jews and half-black girls from Chicago."

"You're messing with me."

STICKY ATOMS

Charlie Mahan was seventeen years old when he was sent to prison for what he did to Julia Bishop.

He went to *grown-up* prison, which is where seventeen-year-old boys who do *grown-up* things get sent.

Some of the inmates at Pontiac Correctional Center called Charlie Mahan Wolfie, because they thought his eyes looked like the Wolfman's.

Charlie Mahan never said one word the entire time he was incarcerated, which caused most of the other men in Pontiac to call him Dummy. Charlie Mahan wrote poetry.

When I hear the word "Pontiac," I think of muscle cars. When I hear the word "correction," I think everything's going to be fine.

:|:

Charlie Mahan was beaten to death three months after arriving at Pontiac Correctional Center.

Atoms will be freed.

. . .

Standing beside one of the pyramidal mounds of pink concrete that had been left behind when twelve billion gallons of water atoms remodeled the St. Francis Dam made me realize just how massive William Mulholland's self-taught failure was.

Julia and I could look up at the canyon rims on either side of us and imagine the towering monolithic face of a one-hundred-fifty-foot-tall death trap that stretched across the sky from west to east.

There were no other human beings here at all; just us and the ghosts.

"If nobody knew this had been part of a dam, you'd just think there were some weird-ass pink boulders here in the canyon," Julia said.

"I read that there had been really tall sycamore trees down here along the creek, and they all ended up in Ventura County, or floating in the Pacific Ocean like broken matchsticks," I said.

There were almost no sycamore trees left in the canyon now, only the fast-growing cottonwoods that sprouted like weeds and formed a thick belt of green to mark the course of what little moisture remained beneath the dry earth at this sweltering time of year.

"It's hot," I said.

Julia said, "Take your shirt off."

"Okay."

I wasn't afraid of anything around Julia Bishop. Off came my T-shirt. The slight breeze felt so cool blowing through the wet hair in my armpits.

"Lazarus Door," Julia said. "You are a fallen angel."

:|:

"Cade makes up disgusting names for it," I said.

"I know."

"It's only a joke," I explained. "I love Cade. I think he's the funniest kid I know too."

"His parents must be on meds," Julia said.

"Um."

Julia and I walked north along the creekbed to a place beyond where William Mulholland's dam had been. We sat down on the rocks in the shade along the dry creek and ate a lunch she'd prepared for us: peanut butter sandwiches and sliced apples.

"People driving through here at night claim to see ghosts, especially at those turns below the power plant," I said.

"Have you ever seen one?"

"I don't believe in ghosts," I answered. "At least, not the way that people who *do* believe in ghosts account for them. I think ghosts are just leftover sticky atoms—stubborn ones that do not want to stop holding on to one another."

"Oh," Julia said.

I went on. "Sticky atoms are caused by love, or sometimes by hate or fear. The knackery has a hard time breaking down love and hate into anything else."

Julia nodded. "It makes sense. I suppose that means it's important to love as much as possible. You know—so the hate that can't get rendered into something else is smaller and weaker that way."

"I believe you understand the physics of the knackery," I said.

We held hands and walked beneath the brilliant green shade of cottonwood trees, back toward the old power plant.

ANDREW SMITH

. . .

There was a lonely and quiet museum entirely devoted to William Mulholland's disaster. The museum was housed in a recycled portable classroom building parked adjacent to Power Plant No. 1.

When Julia and I were inside the museum, the worker there—an acne-faced boy who couldn't have been much older than nineteen and dressed in the green uniform of an Angeles National Forest intern warden—assumed we had come in because we were lost or had witnessed a traffic accident in the canyon, which, he explained, were the two most common reasons why the door to the museum ever opened.

The third most common reason was for mail delivery.

Nobody ever visited the museum, because pretty much everyone on the planet had forgotten all about the St. Francis dam.

I had put my shirt back on before going inside. I didn't want anyone to think the aliens had arrived. Besides, what if I got hungry enough to eat the apprentice-warden kid?

And I probably *would* have eaten the punk too. I did not appreciate the leering way the kid ogled Julia Bishop. And Julia, noticing me noticing the warden-in-training, grabbed on to my hand and squeezed.

"No, we're not lost," I explained. "We are actually interested in the dam."

"What?" Warden Boy said. "There was a *dam* here?"

"Um."

Then the kid burst out laughing.

Good one.

I decided to ignore the asshole from that moment on.

The museum housed a rather eclectic assortment of display items: a scale-model diorama of the predisaster dam and reservoir, handwritten letters and journal entries from survivors, a bent and mangled pressed-tin toy automobile that was unearthed in the rubble, newspaper accounts from 1928, and hundreds of photographs that included scenes of the dam's construction, William Mulholland's life, the aftermath of the collapse, a flattened field littered with dark mounds that turned out to all be drowned horses, and dozens of portraits of the known victims of the St. Francis disaster.

One of them, very disturbing, caught my attention and drew me in.

Here is what the photograph looked like: It was a black-and-white portrait that had obviously been taken in a photographer's studio. There were three children in the picture—two girls standing on either side of a three-year-old boy who was seated on a very ornate enameled cast-iron bench. Behind the three hung a screen on which had been painted the image of a fog-shrouded forest of trees. The boy looked bored and confused, sitting there in short pants and shiny leather shoes with his mouth hanging slightly open. You could almost smell the odor of baby drool on him. His socks were slightly rolled at their tops, and he had on what looked like a sailor's shirt. His name was Danny. He and his mother survived the flood caused by William Mulholland's failure. Barefoot and injured, Danny's mother carried him up the steep canyon wall that towered above their homestead.

The two girls, Danny's five- and six-year-old sisters, died in the early hours of March thirteenth, 1928, along with their father, who worked at the power plant. The sisters had identical bowl-cut hairdos. All the children had perfectly straight corn-silk blond hair.

The sisters' names were Marjorie and Mazie.

And I had seen them before.

I whispered, "Okay. Now I *am* seeing ghosts."

I didn't want Acne Warden Kid to hear me.

Julia said, "What?"

"Those two little girls in this picture," I said. "I saw them standing in my living room the night you found me on the floor."

Sticky atoms.

On our drive home that afternoon, Julia and I talked about Marjorie and Mazie Curtis—the two little girls in the old photograph we'd seen at the St. Francis Dam Museum.

Julia theorized that perhaps the girls felt sad for me, that we had some kind of a kinship because of what had fallen from the sky onto us all, so they were looking out to see if I'd be okay.

:|:

"It's hard to say. Maybe I was mistaken about them being there in my living room. I can't account for anything I see when I start blanking out," I said. "And you don't feel sorry or sad for me, do you?"

"Would it be terrible if I did?" Julia asked.

"I don't know. Maybe."

"You know, it's okay to feel bad about things that happen to people you care about."

"I suppose it's what people are going to do," I decided.

Then Julia said, "I have something for you. I'm going to give it to you on the night before your birthday. It will be a perfectly tremendous surprise."

"Okay. I'm surprised right now," I said.

"But you have to promise to come to my house the night before, at midnight, and stand outside my window and wait for it," she said. "That way, it will happen just during the first minutes of your actual seventeenth birthday."

My actual birthday, two weeks away, was about twenty-four million miles in front of Julia Bishop and me. That was a long stretch to wait while nervously wondering what she intended to give me.

My surprise began to shift toward nervousness. What could a girl like Julia Bishop possibly need me to do at midnight outside her window?

I was terrified it might have something to do with sex. I did not think I wanted to actually *have* sex, despite how frequently I thought I did want to have it. And Julia seemed so worldly to me, like the kind of girl who would think that sex was a perfectly reasonable gift to give a kid when he turned seventeen.

She was the kind of mature and outwardly confident, perfect girl who really *could* have a forty-year-old airline-pilot boyfriend, and you wouldn't think twice about their relationship.

My mind raced. I began to feel flushed with embarrassment at the thought of asking Cade Hernandez to drive me to a 7-Eleven so I could buy a pack of condoms. I began to sweat.

It was ridiculous.

Hurry! Hurry! Step right up and see the epileptic boy try to purchase his first pack of rubbers!

"Can I bring Laika?" I squeaked.

Julia smiled. "If you want to. Just promise you'll come."

When she said that last word, my throat knotted so tight, it felt as though I'd swallowed a horseshoe.

"Um."

I was such an idiot.

And I thought, Cade Hernandez probably has plenty of condoms. I hoped I could save myself the desperation of standing eye-to-eye with some liquor-store clerk as he scanned the price code and waved a box of condoms around for every fucking set of eyes in Burnt Mill Creek to see.

Maybe I could just ask my best friend if he would loan me some.

Loan?

That made me feel sick too.

I moped the rest of the way home, which wasn't too far. Power Plant No. 1 was only six miles up the canyon from my house.

Julia said, "I know what you're thinking."

That terrified me even more. I hoped she wasn't tuned in to the fact that I was actually thinking about having sex with her, and how I could obtain some condoms, and how a guy even *used* a condom in the first place.

I knew enough to never have sex without condoms. Tracy—Mom—had a most awkward talk with me about the subject near the end of last baseball season, during our school's spring break. Mom had been my nurse, after all, and was more intimately familiar with all my most embarrassing atoms than anyone on the planet of humans and dogs. So who better to talk to a sixteen-year-old boy about condoms and sex?

Mom had apparently heard rumors about Cade Hernandez and Monica Fassbinder.

Rumors spread like a diaspora of atoms in the knackery of the universe, always getting rendered into something else and something else.

Mom had methodically explained all the possible consequences involved in having sexual contact without using condoms. She structured her lesson to save all the scariest parts—infections that settle in on the insides of boys' penises and testicles—for the very end. I'm sure Mom was going to have an entirely different "lesson" when my sister, Nadia, turned sixteen or so.

Her one error was in asking if I wanted her to buy some condoms for me. What sixteen-year-old boy would ever say yes to such a question posed by his *mommy*?

It was a lose-lose situation any way you looked at it. But it would have been so much easier for me, I realized as I sat sweating inside Julia Bishop's Ford Mustang, if I had simply told my stepmother *yes*.

Julia nudged my shoulder and added, "But don't even try to guess what it is, because I'm not telling till your birthday."

"Um. Okay."

Julia Bishop parked in the semicircular driveway at the front of my house.

Most of the homes on the east side of the canyon had grand driveways with arching iron gates. My house was gateless.

When we got out of her car, I saw that Mr. Castellan had been standing at the edge of his property, watching us through the metalwork on his fence.

Manuel Castellan not only moved like a gaited horse, but when he stood still, he was like a chameleon—he blended in perfectly with the dry-earth colors of San Francisquito Canyon.

He wagged a finger at me and smiled. "You see, Caballito? This is how things will always go. A boy like you has remarkable taste. And luck, too, I should say!"

Mr. Castellan was quite obviously admiring the girl walking next to me.

"What did he call you?" Julia asked.

"It's my bullfighter name," I explained.

Mom made iced tea for us when we came back from our visit to William Mulholland's great failure. We sat in the living room and did what teenage boys and girls do when they're being observed by one of their parents—fidgeted in awkward silence.

Nadia, being the perfect example of six-year-old-sibling femininity, squeezed herself down on the couch between me and Julia, so she could put her powder-scented hands on both of us.

She does the same thing when Cade Hernandez comes over, but Cade and I generally don't sit with our knees touching. That would be awkward.

Girls always know exactly what they're doing.

I sighed. "Do you really have to sit right here, Nadia?"

My sister patted our legs and said, "Yes. I like Julia too. And I love my big brother."

If Tracy—Mom—hadn't been there, I probably would have fought with Nadia, who was quite obviously calculating some unspoken communication about Julia and me maintaining our physical and emotional distance from each other.

I was not above fighting with my six-year-old sister.

Mom gave the three of us her most contented look. It was like a moment from a television sitcom.

And what can a guy possibly do besides give in when he's all alone in a room with three powerful females?

My brain became a twelve-billion-gallon flood of stupidity. I found myself staring dumbly at the spot on the floor where I'd blanked out and pissed myself the night Julia and I first truly met, while I kept fantasizing in terror what it would be like to climb through Julia Bishop's bedroom window at midnight, nervously strip myself naked, and have sex with her. I replayed in my mind the talk Mom had given me about condoms and sexually transmitted infections inside my penis, and thought about how, later that week, I'd have to talk to Cade Hernandez about everything and ask for his advice.

That was very stupid.

Then Mom said to me, "Did you ask her yet?"

I was horrified. Ask her *what*?

I said, "Huh?"

Mom let out a disappointed breath. "Julia, we're going to have a little party for Finn on the sixteenth. It's his birthday. Mike and I would love it if you could come."

"And me, too," Nadia said.

"Yes. Nadia wants you to come too," Mom agreed.

I was so embarrassed—again. The atoms inside me were busily cranking out all kinds of sticky hormones that day.

But Julia saved me and said, "Oh, Finn did ask me to come, Mrs. Easton. Thank you very much. Of course I'll come."

"Yeah. I asked her," I croaked.

THE DRIVING RANGE

When you think about it, the theoretical science behind the Lazarus Doors in my father's *The Lazarus Door* kind of made sense, and also contributed to the level of outrage and craziness that resulted in reaction to the book.

Here's how it worked: Since the cannibal-angel-aliens lived on a moon so far away from the planet of humans and dogs, blasting their personalized atomic-size doorways out into space would mean that some of the doors would land on Earth before others. And, over so great a distance, just a little bit of "time" would mean that some of the Lazarus Doors would open thousands of years before others.

Look: You know how awkward it is when a lonely, early guest shows up hours before the party is *supposed* to start.

What do you do?

So the book hinted—strongly—at the idea that what the authors of the Bible and the Koran described as angelic *messengers from God* were actually hopped-up, hungry incomers who wanted to rape and eat human beings—and got away with it too!

And, later, that cannibalistic serial murderers, like Jack the Ripper and Boone Helm, the Kentucky Cannibal of the 1850s, were also early party guests who'd arrived before the real invasion began and doors started opening by the hundreds of thousands—right here in the modern era.

Imagine that.

Time gets all messed up when you travel so far through space.

I never do well in situations where I feel like I am in the spotlight of attention. I get ridiculously nervous and confused.

I believe that trait finds its origins in all the months spent in the hospital after that dead horse fell a hundred sideways miles off the Salmon Creek Gorge Bridge and landed on me. People—grown-ups—hovered over me constantly, touching me, feeling me, dressing and undressing me, eyeing me, poking me, bathing me. I always looked at that time in the hospital as being my actual birth, because I remember nothing of my life from before those days.

For all I really knew, I could have come through a Lazarus Door.

A lot of times, I believe I did, and that my dad's book was more about me than he'd ever let on.

"I need condoms," I said. "How do you work up the nerve to just walk into a place and buy a box of condoms?"

Cade Hernandez nearly choked on his tobacco.

"Dude." He coughed. "You fucking *what*?"

I cleared my throat. "I told you."

Cade and I were spending the afternoon hitting golf balls at Vista Driving Range in Burnt Mill Creek. It was the day after my date with Julia Bishop.

We enjoyed hitting golf balls together. I knew it was a safe activity Cade and I could escape to during our summer break, one that didn't make me feel guilty for not inviting Julia Bishop to come along. I needed to talk to Cade, and I needed to do it *alone*.

Julia Bishop did not golf.

Monica Fassbinder had gone back to Germany the week before.

Cade Hernandez had been noticeably edgier.

What could you do? He said he was working more hours at Flat Face Pizza in order to save up for a trip to Germany, where he hoped to scatter as many of his atoms as possible.

I had told him that we'd need to change his nickname now.

It made him very sad.

And Cade had said to me, "You've got soft hands, Finn."

My response to him was this: "I will punch you in the fucking mouth, Cade."

So my announcement at the driving range caused Cade Hernandez to hook his driver badly and send his ball careening into the protective nets at the front of the parking lot.

There was nobody else on the range. The day was too hot for most golfers, so I felt at ease speaking in the open about sexual issues with Cade Hernandez.

"Say that again," Cade said.

"I need condoms," I repeated.

"What do you need condoms for?" Cade asked.

"Um, I need condoms so my sperm does not escape into anyone. I also need condoms to protect my penis against getting a nasty infection inside my urethra and having it spread painfully into my testicles. That is why I need condoms," I explained.

Mom's speech had really sunk in.

"Wow," Cade said. "Is *that* what you use condoms for? Because I was wondering if it was science-fair time or shit like that. What I meant was, do you need condoms for Julia Bishop?"

I kept my chin down. I swung my five-iron. The ball sailed—maybe one hundred-eighty yards. It was a good swing.

"Yes," I said.

Cade spit a brown blob onto the padded Astroturf mat at his feet.

"Shit," he said.

"I was hoping you'd have some extra condoms and could maybe give me a couple so I wouldn't have to go to a fucking store and buy a pack of rubbers," I said.

"There's no such thing as *extra* condoms," Cade explained. "There are only ones waiting in line to be used. It's like waiting for a roller coaster. It's a long time getting to the front of the line, but when it's your turn the ride is always worth it. Duh."

"Um, so—"

Cade Hernandez looked at me for a moment.

Twenty miles.

Then he bent down and placed a range ball on top of the rubber nipple sticking up from his practice tee.

He said, "Have you ever had sex?"

"No."

I watched him when I said it. I never took my eyes off Cade's face. I noticed he looked relieved when I told him that I was still a virgin.

"Did you actually— Um, I mean, did Julia *tell* you to get some condoms?"

I replaced my five-iron and took out a three-wood.

"Well, Julia told me she wanted to give me something special, and that to get it I had to come to her bedroom window the night before my birthday at exactly midnight. What else could that mean but she wants to have sex? But I'll be honest: It's scary to me. I don't know if I actually feel ready to have sex with someone."

I swung. Decent.

Cade said, "Oh."

"Yeah."

Cade sliced his next shot. He was a quivering mass of tightened-up, sticky nerves since Monica Fassbinder left Burnt Mill Creek. And I'd just made things worse for him.

Cade Hernandez was deep in thought, and clearly the last thing on his mind involved the mechanics of a good golf swing.

So I asked him: "How about you? Have you ever had sex with anyone? Well, I mean, with a girl? And not just with her hand?"

Cade Hernandez actually turned red. He wrapped his fingers around the grip of his driver and said, "Yes."

"Monica Fassbinder?" I asked.

"No. Monica's a virgin. Well, technically she's a virgin," Cade answered. "I've had sex with Iris Boskovitch."

Iris Boskovitch had just graduated from Burnt Mill Creek High School. She had been president of the school's Equestrian Club. Anyone who ever saw Iris Boskovitch immediately thought this about her: *That girl's head is shaped exactly like the sign above Flat Face Pizza.*

If I had been chewing tobacco, I would have choked.

Iris Boskovitch?

I said, *"Iris Boskovitch?"*

"Yeah."

"Did you use a condom?"

"Dude. Don't be a dumb fuck. You *have* to use a condom. Only dumb fucks don't use condoms," Cade said.

He swung again. This time he missed the ball entirely.

"I quit," Cade said. "No more driving range for me today."

"Okay." I put my club away too. "Well, do you have any?"

"Yeah," Cade said. "No problem. Whatever. I'll give you a couple rubbers, dude. Happy fucking birthday. I've got some in my truck."

I was so relieved.

I'd also totally ruined Cade Hernandez's day.

I NEED AN EXTRA BAG

"Here," Cade said.

As soon as we climbed into his truck in the parking lot at Vista Driving Range, Cade reached across the cab and pulled open the glove box. He fumbled through the stack of crap that invariably accumulates inside glove boxes and uncovered a strip of individually wrapped condoms. I had never seen packaged condoms like this before.

Oddly, they reminded me of candy.

There were four of them, stuck together in perfect two-inch square, perforated tear-off foil packets that were colorfully labeled in glossy blue print.

Cade detached two of the squares and handed them to me.

He said, "Here are your roller-coaster tickets."

Holding the actual devices in my hands was a little strange. I could feel the contour of the condoms inside each packet, how they squirmed around beneath my pressing fingers because of all the slippery lubricant on them.

I wondered if the lubricant had been derived from the rendered bodies of dead horses.

I also remembered that I'd heard in health class that it was not a good idea to store condoms inside the glove compartment of your car, so I reminded Cade of this fact.

"In health class, they told us that condoms should never be kept in your wallet or in the glove compartment of your car," I pointed out.

"Dude, that's just a conspiracy against horny teenage boys," Cade said. "Where else is a kid going to keep condoms? Just laying around in the open, on display at his parents' fucking house?"

It was a fair question.

I had no idea where I would keep condoms, especially since I didn't drive.

I turned the things over and over in my sweating hands.

"Um. Are they easy to put on?"

Cade Hernandez shook his head and laughed. "You are so fucking dumb, Finn. It's as easy as putting on your socks."

I thought I could handle that.

"Uh, Cade," I said. "I just noticed something."

"What?"

"These condoms have an expiration date on them. They expired two months ago. See?"

It was a frightening thought.

Expired condoms.

What do you do with expired condoms? Expired condoms are like nuclear waste: There's nothing sensible you can do with it.

I held the little packets up so Cade could see the black date stamped across the foil.

"Dude, it's not like milk. They're rubbers. Even milk is still good after the expiration date," Cade argued.

"You drink *expired milk*?"

I was horrified by my friend's disregard for boundaries.

"You are fucking nuts, Finn," Cade said.

He started the truck and turned the air-conditioning on full blast. I needed it. I was sweating like a pig at the front of the slaughterhouse waiting line.

I argued, "I suppose you'd get on that roller coaster even if the car in front of you skipped the tracks and splattered everyone riding in it all over the pavement."

Cade thought about my question.

He said, "Dude, when you've waited a long-ass time and you're finally at the front of the line, you're going to get on the fucking ride. You'll see."

I put the condoms back inside Cade Hernandez's glove box.

"Well, I am *not* going to use expired condoms," I said. "I like my penis just the way it is."

I shut the glove box with a finalizing *click!*

And Cade said, "Fine. I am driving your ass to the 7-Eleven right now, and I am going to make you suck it up, go inside, and buy yourself a box of condoms."

"Uh."

I really did not want to go.

But what could I do? I had already buckled my seat belt on the Cade-Hernandez-is-driving-you-to-buy-some-rubbers ride.

This car was bound to skip the tracks and splatter me hard.

• • •

Markie Rodriguez worked behind the counter at 7-Eleven.

Just my stupid epileptic fucking luck.

Markie Rodriguez had played shortstop for the Burnt Mill Creek High School Pioneers baseball team. He graduated in June. Apparently, selling condoms, Slurpees, and chewing tobacco at a 7-Eleven was the realization of his post–high school ambitions.

Markie was an okay guy, just a little tightly wound and twitchy. You get that way playing shortstop, where it is so easy to make costly mistakes, which are closely related to extinction.

I believed there was something very ironic in the thought of purchasing a box of condoms from our former shortstop.

"Come on," Cade said.

Cade Hernandez grabbed my elbow and walked me toward the counter where the cash register and Markie Rodriguez were located. It felt like I was being arrested, or being taken to get a spanking or something.

I had never been spanked in my life, by the way.

Nobody would ever spank a kid who'd had a dead horse fall on him.

And as Cade dragged me the twelve feet from the doorway to the counter, I glanced around in terror, taking in as many details of my environment as possible.

First, I noticed as we entered the store that according to the height chart on the aluminum frame of the doorjamb that was intended to help people estimate the size of stick-up men, Cade Hernandez was six feet four inches tall.

That's a big robber.

Cade had grown this year.

I also noticed there was a mother and three kids at the back of the store filling up drinks at the serve-yourself refreshment bar. In the center of the store, a sheriff's deputy poured coffee into a tall paper cup, and a couple of brown-skinned men who looked like gardeners stood in front of the open beer box at the end of the aisle that displayed motor oil and pressurized cans of flat-tire-repair foam.

It was as though all of humanity had gathered at this particular 7-Eleven to watch Cade Hernandez force the epileptic boy to shop for condoms.

I was so horrified, I felt like I could vomit.

Never in my life had I considered willing myself into an epileptic seizure, but if I could have wished one to happen, I would gladly have blanked out on the spot. I even considered faking it, but then I looked at the sheriff's deputy and grimly considered what it would taste like if he attempted to perform mouth-to-mouth resuscitation on me.

He had a mustache. And besides, no one wants coffee breath on a hot afternoon.

I attempted to reason with Cade.

That was ridiculous.

"Let's go somewhere else," I pleaded.

"Stop being a little bitch," Cade said.

"Little Bitch is my bullfighting name," I pointed out.

"You are *going* to do this."

Cade tugged me along.

"Ow. You're hurting my arm!"

I sounded like such a baby.

Markie Rodriguez beamed a smile when he saw us in the store.

"Win-Win! Finn! Hey, what's up?" he said.

Without hesitating, Cade said, "We came in to buy some condoms."

I was certain there was not one person in that entire zip code who couldn't hear Cade Hernandez's announcement.

Look: Apart from having had sex with Iris Boskovitch, there was nothing in the world that could ever embarrass Cade Hernandez. So when he had the opportunity to address an audience in such a way as to make every single listener feel somewhat awkward and ill at ease, he was unflinching in his willingness to seize the moment.

Even the two thirsty gardeners standing in front of the stacks of twelve-packs turned their attention to the front counter and the kids who'd come in looking for condoms.

And Markie Rodriguez said, "Um. *We?*"

Markie looked from me to Cade and back to me again. One of his eyebrows drawbridged provocatively.

And Cade, never once reducing the volume of his reply, said, "Well, not *we*. Him. Not that he's the *man* and I'm the *woman*. The condoms are for him and someone else. Who is also not a guy, in case you were wondering. So everything's cool. But Finn needs condoms."

Markie cleared his throat and said, "Glad you cleared that up, Win-Win."

So Cade said, "That kind of gave me a boner. Do you ever get a boner when you talk about sex, Markie?"

Markie answered, "I guess I do. Sure. Who doesn't?"

"Really," Cade said. "It's ridiculous, though. How about you, Finn? Do you ever get a boner when you talk about sex?"

I felt the blood draining from my head. I half expected the shoppers in the store to shower us with outrage. Everyone watched Cade and me in rapt attention. The mother at the drink station nervously told one of her junior-high-school-aged boys to turn around and not look at us. She grabbed the kid's shoulder and spun him to face the ice machine.

I could no longer speak.

And Markie asked, "What kind of condoms do you want, Finn?"

Kind?

There are *kinds*?

"Um."

There were kinds. Just at eye level behind Markie Rodriguez's buzz-cut head, beside a display of Red Man chewing tobacco, hung several rows of various brands of condoms. Markie reached up and started pulling them down one by one, laying the boxes on the counter in front of us.

The sheriff's deputy came up and stood in back of me and Cade. He was ready to pay for his coffee. I wished he would shoot us both.

It was a real dilemma: What do you do? Ask Markie to take care of the deputy first? Make him wait behind the condom shoppers?

Cade held up a box.

"Look at this," he said. "AfterGlow brand. These condoms get hot. Have you ever seen that? Condoms with shit on them that gets hot?"

He was asking his question to the deputy.

The cop shrugged and didn't reply. He was obviously interested but maintained his aloof law-enforcement defense barrier.

Cade went on. "Who would want to put something that *gets hot* on his dick? That's the dumbest thing I ever heard of in my life. Remember that time we put Bengay in your jock, Markie?"

Markie nodded. "That was fucked up."

Then the deputy chuckled. "We did that once, back when I played football."

Cade Hernandez drew a little horizontal triangle in the air between me, Markie, and himself.

"Baseball," Cade said.

The deputy nodded. "Oh. Pioneers?"

"Yeah," Markie said. "Not a good year."

"Hey! You're Cade Hernandez, aren't you?" the deputy asked.

Cade was a very talented pitcher. He'd already been scouted by three major-league teams.

Cade shrugged and nodded.

"So, which one of you guys would want to put burning shit on your penis?" Cade asked.

Nobody answered.

Cade said, "That's what I thought," and put the hot condoms down.

A line stretched behind the deputy. The gardeners each carried cold twelve-packs. The mother and her three kids stood with their drinks. The kids watched their shoes, but their ears flared out like steam shovels.

Twenty miles.

Twenty miles.

My knees shook.

Cade grabbed a different box. "Ultra-thin. Sounds risky, don't you think?"

"Uh," I said.

Although "ultra-thin" did sound risky, I had completely lost the ability to communicate with language.

"Look," Markie offered. "This might be what you want. These condoms have spermicidal jelly on them."

I shook my head. I did not want spermicidal anything. It made me feel sick to think of killing my sperm with jelly.

"I like these condoms in assorted colors," Cade said.

"Lots of guys buy those ones," Markie pointed out.

Two girls from school entered the store. Thankfully, I didn't know their names. They were both about five feet five, though.

"Just give me these," I said. I pointed to a blue box of Trojans. They looked the same as the ones Cade had in his truck.

"Good choice," Markie said.

"An American classic," Cade agreed.

Markie Rodriguez scanned the condoms into the register.

Then Cade said, "Throw in a box of those colored ones for me. The condoms I got in my truck are expired. Only a dumb shit would use expired condoms."

"Smart kids," one of the gardeners said.

Cade looked back at them and smiled. "Thank you. And put a can of Copenhagen in there too, Markie."

"Got it," Markie said.

"Markie," I said, "I'm going to need an extra bag to put over my fucking head."

THE BOY IN THE BOOK

July fifteenth came.

I was so nervous.

It seemed the preceding week had been all a blurry haze. Although I hadn't had a seizure since May, the night of the perigee moon—which was now one hundred million miles behind me—I felt disconnected and drained.

And I was so agitated.

My father noticed it. Everyone did.

"Are you okay, son?" he said to me.

Dad looked straight into my eyes. He could see stuff back there, I was certain. I could tell he was trying to see if maybe I'd blanked out and not told anyone about it. I still felt very guilty for not telling him what had happened to me on the living room floor while he was in New York.

We sat together on the morning of my last day as a little boy, the morning before my seventeenth birthday, drinking our coffee on the patio beside the pool. Laika, freshly bathed the evening before, following a complete body massage on a dead jackrabbit, rested her chin on top of my bare foot.

I said, "I'm okay, Dad."

:|:

"Oh."

Dad sipped his coffee.

He said, "You're not nervous about that college trip with Cade, are you? You know, you don't have to go if you don't want to."

That was Dad's circuitous way of telling me he wished I would stay home forever. Cade and I would be taking our exploratory trip to Oklahoma in just a few weeks. It was time for the epileptic boy to grow up.

"Sometimes I've worried about it. But I think it will be good for me."

"It's one of those things that you're going to eventually do, I suppose," Dad said.

And then I asked him, "Dad, how old were you the first time you had sex?"

Look: Words did not frighten my father. They scared the shit out of me. I almost couldn't believe I'd worked up the guts to ask the question and not choke to death in the process. But words were the atoms in my father's universe, and he was their destroyer and their creator.

Dad put his cup down on the table between us. He glanced over his shoulder. I knew what he was doing. He wanted to see if Mom or Nadia had gotten out of bed and were within earshot.

"*Sex?*" Dad asked.

"Yeah. Well. Um. I mean with someone else."

Somehow I'd just skirted around the issue of masturbation with my dad.

My dad said, "Fifteen. But things were a lot different then."

"Fifteen? What do you mean by *different?*"

"Well, I suppose I mean that you kids now are more mature than I was, that you think about bigger things, and maybe with that maturity there come additional considerations you need to be cautious about," my father explained.

"That sounds like bullshit to me," I said.

Dad nodded.

"It probably is," he said. "Good call, Finn. I just pulled that responsible-dad speech out of my ass. Why did you want to know?"

"Don't you think it's normal for a kid to want to know that about his dad?" I asked. "I can't measure whether I'm normal or not by comparing myself with someone like Cade Hernandez."

I sipped my coffee and watched the undulating surface on the pool.

My dad said, "Are you having sex with anyone?"

I felt myself turning red. I shook my head. I wanted to ask him what he meant by "anyone." "Anyone" is the universe, and that includes an awful lot of people I would never have sex with.

"No," I said. "It just seems like all the guys I know at school have had sex. Everyone has but me."

"That's the biggest high school myth of all time, Finn," Dad said. "Just because the guys say they're doing it doesn't make it true."

I thought about words—like words in books—and how just saying them made things real.

I sighed.

"I think they're telling the truth."

ANDREW SMITH

"Don't worry about it. It's no big deal, Finn. Trust me. Kids make a much bigger deal out of sex than it really is. Don't let anyone pressure you into feeling like there's something wrong with you or you're not normal."

"Wow," I said. "I'm *normal?*"

:|:

My dad laughed. "Probably not."

I put my hand on top of my dad's and told him thanks.

I loved my dad.

He cleared his throat and said, "You know, Finn, when it does happen, just be smart. Normal or not, you're smart."

"Okay, Dad."

All things considered, this was much better than the condom talk with Mom.

I'd hidden the box of condoms Cade forced me to buy between the mattress and the springs on the lower bunk in my bedroom.

Nobody in health class ever advised against that particular hiding place, and since it was my job to do my own laundry, Mom was not likely to stumble onto my secret condoms by changing my sheets.

After dinner, I pouted alone in my room, waiting for the right time to leave. I'd have to sneak out. I'd never left my house that late at night, and if I got caught, there would be questions.

And after our conversation that morning, Dad would know exactly what was going on.

I was scared and embarrassed. I thought about taking off my clothes in front of Julia Bishop—how awkward that would be.

I didn't want her to look at me naked, so, I thought, maybe we could do it in the dark. The problem was, I wanted to see *her* naked. How do the physics of this light/dark fantasy work themselves out for guys, I wondered.

At ten o'clock, I extracted the box of condoms from their hiding place. The box was sealed shut, and I had to unfold the entire thing to read all the detailed instructions printed on the inside. It was all very pharmaceutical, with black-line drawings of how to properly put on and take off a condom.

It was ridiculous.

At eleven, I got dressed and fixed my hair in front of the mirror that hung on the door of my closet. I tried to look good, confident, but I was so unconvincing. I made sure the clothes I wore were all perfectly clean and smelled fresh—shorts, T-shirt, socks, underwear. I wore the socks with the sharks on them, the ones Julia had admired. My briefs were brand-new and had that just-out-of-the-package chemical smell. Thanks, Governor Altvatter! You had to be sure and have fresh underwear and socks if you were going to have sex, right?

Even the laces on my sneakers were never used and brilliantly white.

I was so stupid.

I put two condoms inside my left pocket. How many did you need? I should have asked Cade Hernandez, but he would have put on some theatrical show to answer such a simple question. The instructions inside the box didn't say anything about how many condoms a guy would typically use when having sex.

Two sounded good.

At eleven fifteen, it was time to go. I took my sneakers off so I could get out the back door in my socks without making any noise. Then I realized how dumb it was to call sneakers "sneakers." Those rubber soles were like steel-pan drums on hardwood floors.

I was disgusted with myself.

And just before I left, I turned out the light and put those stupid condoms back inside the box beneath my mattress. Anyway, the expiration date on them wasn't going to hit for another eight-hundred-million miles.

That's a long line for a goddamned roller coaster.

On the way to Julia Bishop's house, I practiced what I would say to her. I used Laika as my stand-in for Julia.

Laika was a good listener, and when I talked to her, she would stay near me and not run off to find something decaying that she could roll on.

It was a win-win situation.

Excuse Number One: *Look, Julia, I really like you a lot. . . .*

Bullshit.

Laika was unimpressed.

Excuse Number Two: *I love you, Julia.*

"Should I say that, Laika? I mean, it's the truth, but I don't think I have the balls to say 'I love you' to Julia until she says it first. Is that totally stupid? I think she's in love with me. Do you think so?"

Bullshit.

Excuse Number Three: *Julia, I am too young and too stupid to have sex. I wanted to believe I could do it, but I can't. I hope you don't think there's something wrong with me, because there's not. I'm just not ready. I love you, and I hope you're not mad at me. I would never have sex without condoms. I even embarrassed myself and bought some, with Cade Hernandez along, no less! Imagine that! And I purposely left them at home tonight because I just don't think I'm old enough to do it yet. Maybe that makes me gay. Maybe it makes me a loser, because all my friends are having sex. Just not me.*

Bullshit again.

It was all true; I just didn't know if I could actually say those words to her.

As I climbed up the bank from the creekbed and onto Julia's property, I found myself wishing I had just stayed home.

There was no light coming from Julia Bishop's bedroom.

Would she even know I was there?

We'd talked about it plenty of times, so it wasn't like either of us had forgotten the mysterious midnight date we'd arranged.

I checked my watch.

Eleven fifty-seven.

Three thousand six hundred miles to midnight.

"Come here, Laika," I whispered.

I folded my legs and sat down in the garden outside Julia's bedroom window. Laika pressed up against my bare thigh, and I patted her fur.

And I said, "You are not running off tonight."

Laika, guilty, hunched her shoulders and sighed.

Flick!

The light on the other side of Julia's window came on.

In the night, the window lit up like a movie screen. It looked odd—a flat yellow cloth of some kind, perfectly clean and smooth with brilliant light shining on it from somewhere inside the girl's bedroom. It was the same color as the moon when you'd see it through the smoke of the bullfighter's incinerator.

Sometimes, you couldn't help but see things through lighted-up windows in the canyon at night. In some ways, living in San Francisquito Canyon was like living in a commune, anyway. Even though most of the people who lived there were hiding from the rest of the world, nobody in that community exerted much effort at all when it came to hiding things from one another.

My father and I were the exceptions. I hid things from him, while he hid things from everyone else.

There is something about the dark of night that makes me feel safer, like I'm not constantly being watched to see if I'm *okay*.

:|:

A shadow moved across the pale screen from the edge of Julia's window frame.

Naturally, I hoped it was Julia. I wished she would come outside and talk to me and make me feel like things were normal, good.

I stared and stared.

The shadow in the window took form.

Act One: The Moon

In the window, I see an ascending circle that rises upward and freezes. It floats just below the upper border of the screen. I can't tell how the object got there—it doesn't seem to make sense. Maybe it is some kind of decoration that dangles from a string. And then the shadow, the circle, begins to eclipse inward. It transforms into a moon. At least, it is the shadow of something that looks exactly like a waning moon in the sky.

Once the shadow reduces to a quarter crescent, it hangs there, motionless.

I watch.

Somehow it makes me feel guilty, like a trespassing thief, but I scoot myself along the ground where I sit, leaning closer to the shadow of the moon and the window of the room where the most beautiful girl I have ever seen sleeps every night.

I stroke Laika and whisper to her, "Do *not* run away."

Act Two: The Door and the Boy

I sit there transfixed as a second shadow figure grows upward from the base of the window. It is a rectangle in black, and once it has settled into place, it shakes silently as though there is some kind of seismic disturbance on the planet beneath the quarter moon. At the edge of the rectangle, a thin slit of light dilates wider. The rectangle becomes a doorway, and it is opening in front of my eyes. Through the illuminated doorway, a new shadow creeps out onto the screen—a slate gray silhouette of a boy who walks across the stage of the window frame beneath the hovering moon.

They are all paper figures—puppets. I have never seen anything like this before.

And there is nobody here at all, except for me.

The shadow-boy walks out through the open door and stands beneath the hanging moon. His legs move with gawky and mechanical articulations, knees bending while his hands hang at his sides. Every slender finger shows against the light. He is clearly wearing shorts, and his bony legs seem almost skeletal while the smooth profile of his face conveys a detached and sad expression.

The boy turns his chin upward, as though he is observing the moon that hangs in the sky of the lighted screen. His hair is all cowlicks and disarranged spikes.

The boy is me.

He looks exactly like me.

Julia Bishop has made me into a shadow.

It is a ridiculous idea, but I remember how once, when I visited her house, I saw her holding paper and scissors, eyeing me against the blank rectangle, and I thought she'd been sizing me up, as if I were some kind of model.

Crazy.

I inhale, almost certain I will smell the sweetness that brought about my dissolution again, but there is nothing.

"Are you in there?" I whisper.

It is a stupid thing to do. I can hardly hear myself setting those words free into the night.

I am so foolishly self-conscious.

Beneath the moon, the boy pauses and looks down at his feet. He raises his hands to the front of his chest.

The earth travels twenty miles per second, and it pulls the moon along through space.

Twenty miles.

Twenty miles.

Act Three: The Tiger and the Book

A larger figure jumps out across the screen. The suddenness of the motion startles me. The new shadow flares claws and teeth. It is a tiger, with slashing lines cut through its body, flashing perfect stripes of light. The shadow-boy lowers himself defensively, like Laika does when she's been scolded.

The tiger-shadow transforms into a man, taller and thicker than the boy. He waves a pointing finger at the boy, as though he is accusing the boy of something, or maybe punishing him, telling him what he must do. When the boy raises his hands away from his chest, he lifts a crown over his head and places it down on top of his messy hair.

The shadow-man points up at the moon, and from the top of the screen, a large square—a book—flutters downward over the figure of the boy and his crown as though eating him between the flaps of its bindings. The boy disappears inside the book.

Then the light inside Julia's room shuts off, and everything is dark.

The screen is erased in blackness.

I push myself up, standing, and whisper, "Julia?"

The light flashes again. The window is entirely dark except for the outlines of block letters, shining, brilliant words that hang between myself and whatever is on the other side of the glass. The words say this:

HAPPY BIRTHDAY, FINN EASTON. I LOVE YOU.

Click!
Darkness.
Show over.
The End.

ANDREW SMITH

So this was what Julia Bishop had intended to do for me in the first moments of my seventeenth birthday, and it was better than anything I'd imagined. I felt so stupid, disgusted with myself for making such idiotic assumptions about Julia, about the way things would be in the miles ahead of us.

I moved so close to her window, I could feel the coolness of the glass on my lips.

"Julia?" I whispered. "Thank you. That was the best present I ever got. I love you."

Her window budged open, just an inch.

"You're welcome," Julia said.

I couldn't see her at all. Her voice might just as well have been coming from outer space.

"I wish I could see you," I said.

"We'll see each other at your party. I can't come out."

"I suppose it would be stupid for me to try to come inside. I'll go home now."

Then Julia Bishop said, "Wait."

The window slid a few more inches, and Julia's face appeared in the opening.

"How does the boy—how do I get out of the book?" I asked.

Julia said, "I haven't seen that part of the story yet."

I pressed my palm against the mesh screen on her window, and Julia's hand met mine. I could not begin to calculate the trillions of atoms separating us, but I had never felt closer to anyone in my life.

"I want to kiss you," I said.

"Tomorrow."

The window slid shut, and Julia disappeared.

Laika was a good dog. She stayed right beside my feet for the long walk home through the canyon's creekbed.

And on my way, I practiced telling Julia Bishop how sorry I was for thinking the wrong thing about her. Laika graciously accepted my apology on Julia's behalf. I could almost hear my dog saying that it was one thing to think incorrectly, but acting incorrectly was a completely different universe, and I hadn't gone there with Julia Bishop.

Dogs get really smart when they've traveled as far through space as Laika had.

"Thank you for not rolling in anything dead tonight," I said.

Laika grinned her tightened rat-terrier grin.

And I thought, maybe everything in the universe is alive tonight, anyway. It felt that way to me.

So I said, "I am seventeen years old. That's almost eleven billion miles."

Then I smelled the honeysuckle-sweet sick odor that told me it was time for Finn to go.

It was ridiculous.

It was unfair.

I howled into the nighttime sky.

"Fuck no! Not now!"

There were lights this way, lights that way, all drifting outward from the center, moving so far and fast as the knackery claimed the words from me and I emptied and emptied, falling, the Little Bitch, Caballito, on my hands with my mouth— what was that?—in the dirt while two little girls named

Marjorie and Mazie stood at the edge of the trees along this dried bank where they died together and sang,

> *One atom at a time,*
> *One atom at a time.*

A PLAY ABOUT THE EPILEPTIC BOY AND ANTS

It was trouble.

My little sister, Nadia, eager to pounce me into wakefulness on the morning of my seventeenth birthday, discovered my bed had not been slept in.

Her brother was missing.

When my atoms trickled back together, the first thing I became aware of was this: *I have dirt in my mouth.*

Everything that slowly congealed into *me* burned like acid from the bites of red ants.

If I had lain there for a few million miles more than I did, the knackery of the ant nest would have disassembled Finn Easton and turned him into all sorts of useful ant products.

It took me thousands of miles to figure out what the burning was. Then I realized my eye had been focused on the jaws of one of the little monsters as it bit into the bridge of my nose.

And I hadn't pissed myself—Dad's little boy was growing up!—because if I had, those goddamned ants wouldn't have wanted to get inside my underwear. As it was, although I could not move, I felt the needled mandibles of each individual ant biting the insides of my thighs, my balls, and my penis.

Where were my arms?

Words crawled back to my head: canyon, morning, Laika, dirt, birthday, and *why is everything on fire?*

My fingers opened and closed.

Laika's ears shot up when I balanced myself shakily over my hands and knees. My head was a vacuum to all the diffused fragments of my universe I'd scattered into the dark on the way home from Julia Bishop's house. Time for Finn to suck it all back in.

I spit sandy mud.

Words filled the space inside me that wasn't already crowded by rage.

The ants were everywhere.

I must have looked insane—tearing at my clothes, stripping them off my body and flailing them like flags of surrender in the cool morning air until I was completely naked, swatting and brushing at my skin, a pale cloud of atoms twitching a pathetic war dance in the bottom of a canyon that was no stranger to crazy ghosts.

Laika ran around in circles, excited and amused by whatever game she thought I must have been playing.

Hurry! Hurry! Step right up and see the naked epileptic boy throwing a fit as he slaps himself silly!

A car drove by on the canyon road.

Anyone could have seen my freak show there in the clear light of morning.

It was ridiculous.

Lowering myself, hunched over like one of those not-quite-bipedal wild boys who'd been raised by wolves or monkeys, I gathered up my discarded clothes. Then I hid inside a cover of cottonwood saplings and made certain every last ant was gone before I put them on again.

I had no idea of the time, the miles I'd traveled since leaving Julia Bishop's window and the shadow play. When I looked around, I could see that I'd ended up halfway between Julia's house and my own.

As was always the case after blanking out, I could not decide which way I was supposed to go.

I went home.

There was nothing I could do. I couldn't run away on my birthday. Dad and Mom would have thrown a fit. And when I showed up at our front door, dirty and stinging with injury, I had no choice but to tell them the entire truth about what had happened to me and how I'd spent my night facedown on a nest of red ants.

The ant bites made me sick. The stinging grew worse with every step on my walk home. So I was nearly hysterical with pain when I told my parents and sister about blanking out, and what I'd been doing in the canyon after midnight.

I went to see a puppet show. They thought I was delirious.

Mom, the nurse—Snow White—told me to take everything off and sit in the bathtub while she ran it full of cool water.

Of course it was embarrassing, but I was in no condition to argue the treatment. Enduring the punishment of sitting naked in a bathtub on my seventeenth birthday in front of my parents was better than having them take me to a hospital, which was the first thing Mom had suggested.

Mom and Dad were angry.

Me? I wanted to drive my fists through the tiled walls in our perfect California bathroom.

I ruined my birthday.

Things could not have been much worse if we'd invited Blake Grunwald over so he could do a German dance, then get drunk, start a fistfight, and puke his guts out all over my bed.

Mom gave me some antihistamine pills after I got out of the bath. The medicine made me feel drunk and dizzy. I couldn't put on clothes; it hurt too much. I went to bed and rolled over between the cool sheets with my face turned toward the wall so I could make everything invisible.

At that moment, I wanted to die. I became a swirling cosmic storm of anger and depression. I wanted to tell Mom to go away, to leave me alone, but I pretended to be a good kid instead, the way Dad would have written it.

:|:

I knew there were a hundred kind and loving reasons why Mom sat in my bedroom and watched me as I lay there, not sleeping, pretending to sleep, wishing so hard that everything would go away, that I could roll the fucking planet back all those miles to yesterday and try to do things better.

Finally, I went to sleep.

Perhaps it was an effect of the pills Mom had given me, but in my sleep I dreamed about riding a flying horse with Marjorie and Mazie Curtis, of fighting bulls in a dusty Mexican arena, of black shadows on the screen in Julia Bishop's bedroom window.

In the evening, Dad came to my room and woke me up.

"Are you going to sleep through your entire birthday?" he asked.

He kept the light turned off. I was grateful for that.

"Apparently not," I said.

I was never very polite after one of those episodes, and that day—my birthday—I felt particularly toxic for the humiliation of having been given a bath by my stepmother.

Look: Here's another thing about my father's book, *The Lazarus Door*: Some of the aliens became epileptics after they'd removed their wings.

Imagine that.

There was almost nothing about me that wasn't in his book, that didn't trap me into being something invented by someone else.

Dad put his elbows on the mattress of the top bunk. I kept my face to the wall, my eyes glued shut.

He said, "Are you feeling better?"

"I haven't felt this good in at least two million miles," I said.

:|:

"How are the teeth marks?"

I didn't answer. How would I know?

Besides, I was being very mean, and I never let anyone off the hook when I felt this way.

166   ANDREW SMITH

So Dad said, "I want to see how you look."
Here is what happened:

The curtain opens on a darkened bedroom. It is the evening of a California summer day. FINN, *a teenage boy, is lying with his face turned to the wall, undressed but wrapped in sheets on the upper of two bunk beds. His father,* MIKE EASTON, *leans over the boy, concerned for him. As the curtain rises,* MIKE *reaches across his son and switches on a goose-necked reading lamp clipped to the rail of* FINN's *bunk bed, uncovers his son's bare shoulders and back, leans over him, and rubs the boy's skin where he had been severely bitten by ants.*

MIKE: Looks like the bites are pretty much gone.

FINN: That's good.

MIKE: So. Nobody ate yet. We were waiting on the barbecue to see if you'd make it down. Cade's here. Um. Please tell me you're not going to make me sit down to dinner with Cade Hernandez as the only other male in the house, son.

FINN: Is Julia here?

MIKE: Yes.

FINN: Ask her how I get out of the book. I need to know.

MIKE: *(Puts his palm on the boy's forehead. He thinks his son is delirious from the seizure and the ant bites)*: You feel a little hot. Maybe you should just stay in bed.

FINN *(Shakes his head and sits up)*: I wouldn't do that to you. Let me get dressed. And fix my hair or maybe shave or whatever, since you think I need to start doing that, and I'll be down in a few minutes.

MIKE *(Pats the boy's shoulder)*: Happy birthday, Finn.

FINN: Yeah. Happy birthday, Dad. *(Pauses)* Dad, I didn't actually come through a Lazarus Door, did I?

MIKE *(Exhales a long breath)*: I'm sorry you have to put up with the things you go through, Finn. I wish I could make it all go away. If I could give you one present, it would be that.

FINN: I feel like I'm in the book and I can't get out of it. I feel like everything I've ever done and everything in all those miles ahead of me have already been determined and there's nothing I can do that will change anything.

MIKE: It's not you, Finn. Everyone feels trapped sometimes. Everyone feels unsure of where they came from, how they got here. But none of that really matters, does it? Don't you know that right here, right now, you are the most important person to me in the world?

FINN *(Shakes his head)*: I wish I could be sure.

MIKE: Everyone wants to be sure, son.

FINN: Did you ever feel this way?

MIKE *(Laughs)*: I always feel this way.

FINN: Do you think I'm normal?

MIKE *(Nods)*: I think you're perfect.

FINN: I'm sorry, Dad. I'll straighten up. Just give me a few minutes. Like, four thousand miles or so.

MIKE: Okay. Happy birthday.

FINN: Sure thing.

MIKE *leans over and kisses the top of* FINN's *head.* FINN *lies down, rolls over, and faces the wall again.* MIKE *shuts the door as he leaves the bedroom.*

    (*Curtain.*)

    It was ridiculous.

For my birthday, Cade Hernandez gave me a belt made from an old fire hose, and a brass statue of a bullfighter.

He'd had the base of the statue engraved with the following:

Mom and Dad didn't get it. They had horrified looks on their faces. They were appropriately embarrassed at the likelihood of my little sister, Nadia, seeing the inscription.

This was Cade Hernandez in perfect form.

"How thoughtful of you to remember my bullfighter name," I said.

Cade Hernandez, who'd given me the socks with the sharks on them—the ones I wore the day Julia Bishop first noticed me at Burnt Mill Creek High School—had a knack for choosing the coolest gifts.

And throughout the evening of my birthday, Cade kept looking from me to Julia with the eye of an interrogating detective, no doubt trying to determine what might have happened between us the night before.

Eventually, I did tell my friend the entire embarrassing truth.

THE LAKE THAT ISN'T A LAKE

The Perseid Meteor shower commonly peaks in early August. The spectacle, created by the slow disintegration of the comet Swift-Tuttle, is named for the constellation Perseus, the Greek hero who killed Medusa.

Just a bit more than two weeks, around twenty-four million miles, after my seventeenth birthday, the Perseids scattered brilliant torrents of blazing dust all across the nighttime sky.

The knackery put on a real show.

Although I'd asked her a number of times, Julia continued to insist she did not know how her shadow story might end, and that we would have to see what happened in the miles ahead of us.

I was desperately in love with Julia Bishop.

I suppose love, which makes atoms sticky, is also in many ways a prison.

Mom and Dad were less than enthusiastic about allowing their epileptic son to leave for an overnight campout adventure in the desert with Cade Hernandez and Julia Bishop. But in the end they decided to loosen the grip they had on their seventeen-year-old boy.

Cade and I were road-tripping for our visit to Dunston University the following week, so I suppose I was testing my limits with my parents and trying to spend as much time as possible with Julia before going away.

I promised to take Laika along as chaperone to restrain any potential recklessness on our part.

Mysteriously, as was so frequently the case with her, Julia Bishop said she wanted to tell me something. I supposed I knew what it was—that she would tell me the end of the shadow story, if the boy was ever able to get away from the book—but I also recognized my very poor record at guessing what Julia Bishop actually had in mind. So I tried to push all those assumptions about escape and sex and stars and planets out of my head.

We were going out for a night, just to have fun, to watch the Perseids from a place where there was no pollution from the light that escaped furnaces like Burnt Mill Creek and Los Angeles.

After the awkward but inevitable argument with Cade Hernandez, it was decided before we left Julia Bishop's house that I had to sit in the backseat with Laika and that Julia would ride up front with our driver.

What else could I do?

Besides, I'd been feeling sorry for Cade's loneliness since the end of the school year and the absence of Monica Fassbinder.

Cade drove us north through San Francisquito Canyon, and then east into the middle of the Mojave Desert, following a grid of arrow-straight two-lane highways to a place where Cade Hernandez would sometimes come to ride dirt bikes. He had frequently invited me along, but I had no desire to have my back broken again.

Mom and Dad were always completely opposed to the idea of ever allowing me on one of Cade Hernandez's motorcycles. This time, there was no motorcycle in the bed of Cade's truck; only our tent and camping supplies, coolers of food, and undoubtedly plenty of chewing tobacco and beer.

Cade steered with his knee. In one hand, he held a paper cup from Flat Face Pizza. It was his road spittoon. The other hand rested lazily at the twelve o'clock position on the steering wheel, pointing one finger up the road at an old splintered sign.

"This is where we're going," Cade said. "Aberdeen Lake."

"Aberdeen Lake" sounds romantic and mysterious, like it might be located somewhere in the Scottish Highlands, as opposed to an abandoned outpost at the edge of Death Valley.

The sign was hardly readable. It leaned badly and was pocked with bullet holes peppering its surface. Cade pulled the truck off the highway, and we all got out to stand there in the blazing heat of the desert while Julia Bishop snapped photographs of us. Cade and I posed like brave explorers beneath the sign.

The billboard said this:

TURN HERE! VISIT BEAUTIFUL ABERDEEN
LAKE—A RESORT OASIS IN THE CALIFORNIA DESERT!

MODELS NOW OPEN!

The sign showed a woman in a light blue one-piece bathing suit, apparently grasping a towline from a speeding motorboat.

She was sailing along on a pair of water skis that fanned rooster tails beyond the edge of the sign. The skiing woman, blond and pale skinned, the iconic model of postmodern femininity, was smiling and wearing sunglasses.

I guess the exclamation points said it all.

Excitement.

The turn you would take, if you obeyed the sign, led down a rock-strewn road that transformed into an angry river during desert flash floods. And that was exactly the road Cade Hernandez drove us on to get to his secret camping spot near a forgotten place called Aberdeen Lake.

By evening, we had set up our camp along the edge of an enormous crater—a hollowed-out earthen swimming pool half a mile across that would have been the lake for Aberdeen Lake. It had probably been designed by a self-taught civil engineer, which may have accounted for the absence of all those expected molecules of water.

Our camp consisted primarily of a dome tent that was large enough to stand up in. We all had sleeping bags too. I felt nervous about the sleeping arrangements, though, and doing things such as dressing and undressing, or going to the bathroom.

As usual, the epileptic kid was thinking too much.

At night, we sat outside on folding chairs and watched the light show in the sky above us. Cade was very drunk and chewing tobacco, too. He tried to talk us into joining him, but neither Julia nor I would drink, and we certainly weren't going to chew tobacco. Julia and I sat close enough that we could hold hands as we watched all the stars that tumbled out of and into the black overhead.

"What if every one of those is a Lazarus Door?" Julia asked.

"Then we'll be eaten by the ones that don't end up on shitholes," I answered.

"Not you. Not if they see your back," Julia said.

Look: It may spoil the ending, but in my father's book all the incomers except for one—a boy—end up being killed by determined human mobs.

The atoms of the unwelcome visitors were freed.

The boy-alien's name happened to be Finn.

:|:

Imagine that.

It could have been true. Who could say otherwise?

And at the end of the book, which is the biggest reason why people had been hounding my father to write more, doors and doors fall like the scatterings of the comet Swift-Tuttle all over the planet of humans and dogs, while Finn—the alien-boy, not me—tries his hardest to simply fit in and become human and eat regular stuff like cheeseburgers and pizza instead of his classmates.

So the book offered a sad ending for Finn—the alien-boy, not me—who only wanted to feel like a regular human teenage boy and do regular human teenage-boy things, like chew tobacco, maybe, or get hand jobs in a custodian's shed from well-funded German foreign exchange students.

You know, stuff like that.

In any event, my father told me throughout my life that he only *named* the incomer boy after me (and the Mark Twain character); that the Finn in his book was never supposed to actually *be* me.

I suppose that sometimes books imitate life.

And sometimes books imitate lives that imitate books.

Maybe that's why Julia Bishop could not tell me if her shadow Finn could escape from her shadow book. Because despite my father's constant assurances, it was me—this Finn and not the incomer one—who just couldn't feel like a regular kid, like I belonged here.

Twenty miles.

Twenty miles.

Twenty miles.

Cade spit and drank, spit and drank.

Laika snored lightly from inside *Sputnik 2*.

Cade Hernandez got up and walked to the edge of the empty crater. He stood there and peed into Aberdeen Lake.

We dragged our sleeping bags out from the tent so we could lie on our backs and watch the atoms being freed in the knackery above us until we fell asleep.

Cade, predictably, was the first one out of his clothes. He stripped down to his underwear and then lay there on top of his bag with an open beer beside his pillow and a fresh wad of chewing tobacco tucked into his lower lip.

Self-conscious, as always, I sat down on my sleeping bag and slipped off my shoes and socks.

"There's no scorpions or shit like that out here, are there?" I said.

"Mmm. Probably are," Cade said.

So I put my shoes on top of my camp chair. Then I took off my shorts and T-shirt and wriggled into my sleeping bag.

I was so disappointed. Somehow, I'd managed to miss seeing

Julia Bishop undress. I had no idea what she'd done to prepare herself for sleep. It was like magic. Before I knew it, she had slid into her sleeping bag and was lying right beside me.

Julia Bishop was like an undressing, sleeping-bag ninja.

And I'll admit this: I was so turned on thinking about lying in my underwear next to Julia Bishop, even if Cade Hernandez was bound to ruin it—which he did in about two hundred miles, ten seconds. Still, he didn't seem to notice when Julia slipped over and snuggled against me inside my sleeping bag.

We kissed.

It was the most perfect sensation I had ever felt—Julia Bishop's long, smooth legs tangled with mine while we kissed. I put my arms around her, and she held on to me.

If my heart jumped out of my chest, it would take off through space faster than the earth itself. Of course Julia had to have been aware of exactly how aroused I was. There was nothing I could do to hide it, and I was embarrassed, but only a little.

Everything about the moment felt too good.

Twenty miles.

Twenty miles.

Then Cade sat up and said, "Have you two ever had sex yet?"

I groaned.

"Shut up, Cade," I said. "I told you already. No. I am too young and too stupid for something like that."

Cade took a long drink. He sat in his briefs, cross-legged on top of his sleeping bag, watching us. He turned away and spit a big blob of tobacco.

Splat!

"Well, I have," Cade announced. "I'm no virgin."

"I know," I said. "You told me. You're drunk. Remember? Iris Boskovitch."

Julia whispered to me, "The girl with the *round head*?"

I nodded a confirmation.

Cade took another drink. He crawled on his hands and knees toward the coolers. At first, he attempted to get a beer from Laika's *Sputnik 2*, then he laughed and said, "Shit."

Pfft!

Cade Hernandez opened a beer.

Wobbling, he stood over us. "Not just with Iris Boskovitch. I also . . . Hey! Are you two *in bed* together?"

"Shut up, Cade. We're just lying down. I promise we are not going to have sex," I said. "Why don't you go back to bed and watch the meteors?"

"Shit, Finn. That kind of gives me a boner."

"Um."

Cade sighed and went back to his sleeping bag. He sat down heavily and took another drink.

He said, "Did I ever tell you about the time I went to a sperm bank to try and sell my sperm?"

I cleared my throat and shifted nervously. I was getting hot and was afraid I would sweat on Julia, which was kind of disgusting—getting all that moisture on her.

I said, "Uh. No."

"Well, I did. You know how much a guy can make selling sperm? You can make, like, three hundred bucks a week. Dude. I have an endless supply. I could break that fucking bank. I'd never have to work a day in my life."

Cade Hernandez tilted his head back and guzzled beer. His eyes gleamed with pride and horniness.

"But they told me I had to wait until I was eighteen. Dude, do you realize how much money's worth of sperm I'm going to be wasting between now and next April?"

Cade Hernandez was an Aries.

"I imagine less than you suspect, now that Monica Fassbinder is about six thousand miles away," I theorized.

Cade went on. "Shit. I can't stop it. Who can? I'm a fucking fountain of expensive sperm. But anyway, I didn't only have sex with Iris Boskovitch. You know who else I had sex with? Just try and guess."

I didn't need to say anything. When Cade Hernandez was in this particular form, I knew he was certainly going to answer his own question.

So he did.

Cade Hernandez said, "Mrs. Shoemaker."

Julia laughed—a gasping, startled kind of giggle.

I said, "You had *sex* with our *substitute teacher*? What is *wrong* with you, Cade?"

Like a lot of boys I knew, I often wished that some of Cade Hernandez's wrong magic would rub off on me. But Mrs. Shoemaker wasn't only a substitute teacher, the one who'd taken over for Mr. Nossik after his unfortunate aneurysm, she'd also been Monica Fassbinder's host mother.

"Well," Cade explained, "it wasn't at school or anything weird like that. Um. In fact, it was during summer vacation, so that makes her technically not a substitute."

"I guess you're off the hook, then," I said.

Cade said, "It happened on the day we drove Monica to the airport to go back to Germany. After we dropped her off. When we got home, Mr. Shoemaker volunteered to go out to get us hamburgers. Mr. Shoemaker is such a nice guy, isn't he? As soon as he left, Mrs. Shoemaker grabbed my hand and led me into her bedroom. She was looking at me weird the whole day. I kind of knew what she was thinking. You know how you can tell, it's so obvious when someone's looking at you like they want to have sex with you?"

I will admit it: I did not know what someone looked like when they wanted to have sex with you.

I said, "Um. No, Cade. What does it look like?"

And Cade said, "Look at me."

I looked at Cade Hernandez. He was staring into my eyes and had a very contented, almost half-smiling expression. It creeped me out, and I had to look away.

"Uh," I said.

"It looks like that, dumbass. Anyway, I felt guilty about having sex with Mrs. Shoemaker. And the hamburgers were really good. I'm probably going to go to hell for that shit, aren't I?"

Julia laughed. "No doubt you're going to hell, Cade."

"Or you are going to get an infection inside your urethra that will spread like a slow-burning fire into your testicles, and then your penis is going to fall off," I added.

Cade thought for a while and said, "That would be way worse than going to hell."

I had to agree.

It would be worse than going to hell.

"Well, I hope you had the good sense to use a condom," I said.

Cade took another drink. "I did. Uh. But they were expired. Remember those ones I had in my glove box that day at the driving range? When you asked if you could borrow some condoms from me and then you saw they were a couple months out of date? Well, it was one of those I had in my wallet that day with Mrs. Shoemaker. Well, two of them, actually. We did it twice before Mr. Shoe came back with the hamburgers."

Cade Hernandez was obviously not a good student in health class. Here was the trifecta of condom errors: glove compartment, wallet, expired.

The whole married-woman thing was a matter for ethics, which they do not teach teenage boys at Burnt Mill Creek High School.

"Um."

Julia turned onto her side. Her face rested on my bare shoulder, and her hand lay flat on my chest.

She said, "Why did you ask Cade for some condoms?"

"Don't worry," Cade said, "Finn and I went to 7-Eleven and bought some fresh ones."

"Uh." I desperately wanted to change the subject. "Why would you call anyone you had sex with 'Mrs.'? *Mrs. Shoemaker?*"

"I think it's kind of hot," Cade said. "'Mrs. Shoemaker.' Don't you think that's hot?"

I was so confused and agitated. My atoms swirled and vibrated at Julia's touch. She pressed against me, waiting for me to tell her the entire dumb story about the day Cade Hernandez and I went shopping for "fresh" condoms together at 7-Eleven.

And I thought about Mrs. Shoemaker, our substitute teacher, so I answered my friend with the following: "No. No, I do not think calling someone you had sex with 'Mrs. Shoemaker' is hot, Cade."

"Cade," Julia said, "tell me about the time you and Finn went to 7-Eleven to buy condoms. That sounds like a good story."

"It's not," I grumbled.

It was ridiculous.

And it was too late. While we lay there, watching the fragments of Swift-Tuttle burning and fizzing across the black of the desert night, I had to endure the entire humiliating tale. And then I had to confess to Julia how stupid and immature I had been on those days leading up to my birthday.

To make matters worse, for the second time that evening in front of Cade Hernandez, I had to reassert my belief that I was too young and too stupid to have sex with anyone.

I hoped it would all be forgotten, considering how drunk my friend was, so I urged him to have another beer.

And Cade said, "I'll only have one if you drink one with me, Finn."

"Uh. Okay."

Cade got up from his sleeping bag and pulled two beers from the cooler.

Julia leaned to my ear and whispered, "I think you're a good person, Finn. I love you. And it was a funny story."

She kissed the side of my face and rolled onto her back, watching the sky.

Before I could answer her, I heard the *pop! pop!* as Cade Hernandez opened each beer. Then, wearing nothing but a pair of white cotton briefs, he sat down in the dirt beside me and Julia.

"Cheers," he said.

"Cheers."

We tapped cans together.

"You know what's out there?" Cade said.

"A bunch of fourteen-billion-year-old shit and a big fucking knackery," I said.

I was just a little irritated by my friend.

"No." Cade spit again and pointed north, past the front end of his truck. "Not up there. Out that way. There's an empty prison. Did you know that? Aberdeen Lake State Penitentiary. Did you know that? An empty fucking prison."

In fact, I did not know that.

We sure found out, though.

WELCOMING THE ALIENS

Aberdeen Lake State Penitentiary was shut down in 1981 after a riot that lasted for three weeks. Three weeks is about thirty-six million miles. Dozens of inmates and corrections officers died in the riot. It must have been like a little war, an out-of-control knackery all safely encased within concrete and razor wire.

Cade Hernandez dunked his entire head into the freezing mix of ice cubes, water, and empty beer cans sloshing in the cooler beside Laika's *Sputnik 2*.

He screamed.

It sounded like he was being murdered. I sat up in my sleeping bag. It was morning in the desert, and Julia had already gotten out of bed and was boiling coffee on a propane stove we'd set up on the tailgate of Cade's pickup.

Cade said, "That's how you take a camping bath in the middle of the desert."

As the water dripped from his hair, he rubbed it into his armpits and over his chest.

Then he said, "You want to take one, Finn?"

"Um. I don't think that's necessary."

"Dude. You are such a little bitch."

"I know that. It's my bullfighter name, remember? Also, I need to pee."

And that was the day Julia Bishop, Cade Hernandez, and I broke in to Aberdeen Lake State Penitentiary.

Nobody breaks *in* to a prison.

In the morning light, I could see we'd been camped out in the middle of a prestamped, formatted pattern of concrete slabs—the intended foundations for a stillborn community of never-built homes that would have been named Aberdeen Lake.

If the homes had been built, there would have been a real lake, too, one with water in it instead of a couple of kids' piss and a bunch of trash blown on the wind. The lake had been formed and dug to a uniform depth of nine feet, with small wooden boat docks fingering out from its waterless shores where the most desirable concrete slabs had been poured.

I pulled on my T-shirt and shorts and released Laika from *Sputnik 2*. Then I hid on the other side of Cade's pickup so I could pee into that starved lake.

Julia took more photographs while we sat and had coffee. And Cade announced, "We're going to have fun today. Let's poke around inside that old prison and mess with shit before we go home."

"You mess with shit every day," I said.

Cade nodded. He couldn't argue with that.

And Julia said, "I bet that prison's haunted."

"If there was ever a place more prone than a prison to having sticky atoms hanging around, I wouldn't know what it would be," I said.

"A collapsed dam, maybe," Julia said.

Cade stood up suddenly, as though he'd been stung.

"I have an idea," he said.

Cade dug around in the jumble of gear thrown into the bed of his truck. Eventually, he pulled out a can of fluorescent spray paint he'd lifted from an unattended public-works survey truck a few months before.

Cade said, "Come on," and took off down the shore of the empty lake.

Cade Hernandez's idea was this: He wanted to spray paint a message on sixteen of the sun-bleached foundations at the non-existent resort community of Aberdeen Lake.

On one of the most desirable streets, which was actually not so much a street as a gravelly span of dried weeds that gapped a swath of abandonment between one side and the other, we wrote out on the foundations—eight on each side of what was supposed to have been called Lakeside Drive—the following message:

:|: W-E-L-C-O-M-E,

A-L-I-E-N-S-! :|:

The exclamation point said it all: Aberdeen Lake was the place for fun!

ANDREW SMITH

Just in case anyone was looking for a good, flat place to land.

Cade said, "This is to fuck with all the crazies in the world."

"There are enough of them," I said.

And Julia Bishop took pictures of us.

The paint was fluorescent orange. You couldn't help but see it from outer space.

After breakfast, we hiked out across the hardpan of the lake bottom. We headed toward Cade Hernandez's promised abandoned prison.

Trash and old charred fire rings peppered the bottom of the never-filled lake. Dirt-bike riders came here in the cool seasons and camped down in the bed of Aberdeen Lake, where they found minimal shelter from the blasting sundowner winds that came to the desert late afternoons every spring and fall.

So here were countless empty propane canisters, cigarette butts, discarded condoms, beer cans, a nylon sleeping bag that looked like someone had taken a shit on it—all the usual stuff you'd expect from city scumbags who didn't care what they left behind, or what they slept next to.

Cade wore a nylon backpack carrying some water bottles, tobacco, a flashlight, candy bars, a few tools, and our phones. Laika followed along, enthusiastic about the mission to explore the abandoned prison.

At the opposite shore, we sat on the edge of a dry-rotted wooden boat dock and dangled our feet over the Mars surface of the dead lake, which was nine feet below us. Cade and I took off our shirts, and we shared a bottle of water with Julia. And Laika came skittering proudly down the dock carrying something that looked like rope in her teeth.

Laika had found a dead snake.

Dead snakes do not stink like dead mammals. The one Laika found was dried and flat, an old rattler that had become an S-shaped band of snake jerky.

"Put that down!" I said.

Laika, who for whatever reasons had an excessively guilty conscience, immediately dropped the snake and curled up in her "please don't kill me" pose.

I had never hit my dog in my entire life.

"Dumb dog," I said.

I got up and kicked the snake carcass off the dock.

And Cade Hernandez, his stiffened index finger aimed at my back, said, "A double-pierced vagina."

:|:

"Ew," Julia said.

"Yeah. Good one, Win-Win."

"I try," Cade said.

At least I was off the hook for the rest of the day. Cade Hernandez never created more than one title for my scar on any given day.

By noon, Julia, Cade, and I arrived at the prison's outer fence.

There was something incredibly foreboding about the place—massive and silent, adorned with the empty black frames of barred or meshed windows and broken-down metal doors. Jutting up squarely from the quiet desert, butted against rust-colored mountains of tumbled boulders, it was something that would have terrified me if I were there alone. Cade Hernandez and Julia Bishop made everything different.

Three separate rings of fencing surrounded Aberdeen Lake State Penitentiary. Most of the fence lines tilted drunkenly but still retained their intimidating character. Although the fence perimeters sagged and slanted here and there, we still had to use heavy wire cutters to open small doorways in each ring of chain-link for the four of us—counting Laika—to enter the prison grounds.

Cade cut holes for us in each layer of concentric perimeter fencing, and we were in.

We had broken in to prison.

On the inside, we paused for a moment for Julia to snap trophy pictures of all of us, and Laika, too. She propped her camera on a five-gallon-size rumpled jerry can that at one time contained cooking oil, and set the timer.

Our little group of explorers posed. Julia held Laika and stood between me and Cade, both of us shirtless with our arms around her. Cade messed with me during the photograph. He sensually rubbed his fingers on my forearm, and I slapped his hand.

We entered the prison yard near a corner of the main structure, beneath a guard tower that stuck out from the outer walls like a castle's turret. As close as we stood, I could see how dilapidated the prison had become over the decades. The outer layer of plaster had peeled and flaked away from most of the building, showing ancient red-brick walls that were absolutely straight, rising up higher than twenty feet from the yard.

Atop each corner of the cell-block's wall, rounded guard towers seemed to sag sadly at their edges as though the prison itself had exhaled a final dying gasp. And all along the rooftop of the structure stood twelve-foot-tall steel posts, a picket line of uppercase *Y*s, each of them strung with razor wire.

Here, just below one of the guard towers in the yard's corner, the prison designers had installed a basketball court. I suppose there had been some confident belief in the rehabilitative effects of playing a good American team sport. The concrete of the court was cracked everywhere, as though an army of robot jackhammers had trampled through. Sprouting up from every one of the broken faults in the basketball court grew giant weeds and sticker bushes as high as our waists.

Cade and Julia followed me around toward the back of the yard.

We looked for a way to get inside the cell block.

Around the far side of the prison, rows of windows were stacked three stories high in straight floors, forty-five cells to each side of a tier. I counted them. The windows were barred and narrow, which gave the prison building the appearance of being much taller than it actually was. Every window on every floor had been broken out. Some of them had no glass remaining inside their frames at all; others looked like mouths with jagged teeth.

In the center of the bottom tier, a black doorway—a main entrance—sat open. There had obviously once been some sort of stairway or porch at the threshold, because the bottom of the doorway was at least four feet higher than the ground where we stood.

There was junk everywhere in the yard.

Jumbled piles of debris that had once been fixtures and conveniences inside the prison lay scattered all over the grounds. Nearly all of the garbage was buried beneath old yellow foam pads that used to serve as the innards for the inmates' mattresses. Cade found an old wooden pallet and tipped it up to the bottom of the doorway so we could use it as a ladder and climb up into the cell block.

Julia took some more pictures at the open doorway before following us into Aberdeen Lake State Penitentiary.

Being in the prison was as much like stepping inside the carcass of a dead dinosaur as I could ever imagine.

"This is spookier than shit, Finn," Cade said.

"Why are you whispering?" I whispered.

"What if someone's here?"

"Someone *is* here—us," Julia answered.

Laika didn't seem worried at all, but then again the place probably had that pleasant reek of death which so satisfied my dog's finely tuned sense of smell.

The doorway we'd come through must have been some kind of receiving entrance for the lower floor of the cell block. There were small officelike windows on both sides of a short hallway, with triple sets of barred doors, all left open, that led out to the T of the lower tier's walkway.

This was where the new arrivals had come in to Aberdeen Lake State Penitentiary.

Before the third and final set of sliding iron gates, a large tiled room opened off to our right. It looked eerily similar in design to the boys' locker room at Burnt Mill Creek High School, except this one was just a little more battered and abused.

The place had not aged well. Many of its atoms had scattered away.

In fact, the entire prison emitted a distressed kind of fog, like a lingering odor from all the terrible things that had happened there.

You could almost feel all the sticky atoms.

The floor of the room was smoothed concrete; dusted everywhere with flakes and chips from the painted plaster that had peeled away from the top of the walls and the ceiling. Glossy black and beige tiles lined the lower two-thirds of the surrounding walls, creating a backsplash of sorts that was higher than the top of my head. It was as though the room had been designed to be hosed out for efficient cleaning.

"I couldn't imagine how horrible it would be to wind up stuck in a place like this," Julia said.

At the back of this room, a row of thin metal slots looked out onto the main hallway of the cell block. Each of the two opposing side walls were lined with galvanized shower nozzles, and a row of squat and lidless concrete toilets.

Not a very nice place.

Cade stepped through all the crap on the floor and peered out between the slats in the far wall.

He said, "This place is amazing."

Julia clicked off some more photos, then walked out into the hallway. Cade and I pissed into one of the old toilets.

"It must suck being a girl," Cade said.

"Uh."

I kicked the toe of my tennis shoe against the metal flush button sticking out from the tiles behind the toilet. No water came, but the thing moaned a groaning squeak, like a cat that had been stepped on.

And Cade said, "Remind me to take a shit in here before we leave."

I said, "Yeah. I'll do that for you."

I walked back out into the hallway. Julia and I stepped through the third set of jail doors, toward the open hall beneath the tiers.

Laika ran out to the wide main floor of the lower tier, and when Julia and I followed her, Cade Hernandez played like he was going to shut the iron barred door behind us to lock us inside, but he couldn't move the thing.

Apparently, somebody had had the foresight to weld those entry doors permanently open.

I said, "Don't be a dick, Cade. My dad would hate you more than he already does if you accidentally killed me and Julia."

"Good point," Cade agreed.

It looked as though a tornado had blown through the main floor of the cell block.

The center of the hallway rose upward, creating a massive atrium with shattered glass skylights that cut through the roof forty feet above. Each of the two upper tiers had been built so they staggered outward, reversed stair steps. I imagine this was to provide some degree of protection for the people below in case there was anything—or anyone—thrown down from above. Aside from the architectural safety, there was also what looked like a chain-link net that ran the entire length and width of the building, now stretched and sagging across the bottom of the uppermost tier's walkway.

Upon this net lay a jumble of artifacts—desks, chairs, metal bunk-bed frames, clothing, tables, books, shoes, even a sink basin. Looking up at the constellation of garbage, it was as though gravity had abandoned the place and all that junk simply floated, magically free, above our heads.

Julia took more pictures, and Cade said, "Holy shit, you guys. This is amazing."

As much trash as there was thrown out onto the net above was matched and surpassed by the quantity of broken and discarded stuff that had been scattered all along the floor in front of us.

Laika sniffed and ran from pile to pile.

This was heaven for my dog. She stopped and watched me with guilty eyes as she hunched her back and took a shit beneath one of the circular molded table-and-bench arrangements bolted in place to the prison's main floor.

Most of the cell doors stood open. Like the three gates at the receiving entrance, the doors were large rectangles of rounded steel bars that slid on rolling tracks. Each cell was identical: four feet wide, about eight feet deep, concrete and steel toilet, sink, steel-slatted bunk beds.

Black numbers had been stenciled above every doorway: 75, 76, 77. . . .

Cade and Julia walked away from me, down the length of the corridor where the block made a right-angle turn to the left.

Julia held her camera to her eye.

Cade snapped a can of tobacco between his fingers.

Flowers.

I smelled flowers.

"Uh. Cade . . ."

I instinctively moved my hand to try grabbing anything so I might steady myself, but there was nothing to hold on to.

It is the story of my life.

:|:

And everything vaporized into the nameless chaos of my twenty-miles-per-second universe.

Why would I even care about it?

I have a dim recollection of something I doubted could be real. It was this: I wondered why Cade Hernandez and Julia were running toward me, away from where they'd been standing, asking me something—if I was okay.

:|:

And following my friends, I believed I saw Marjorie and Mazie Curtis—the girls who'd been killed in William Mulholland's 1928 flood.

Shadow puppets.

The words were all evaporating at the time, but I was certain in my mind that ghosts had been there in the prison with us all along.

Imagine that.

Crazy.

Look: How can I ever describe the wordless universe I enter at times like these, and do it on paper, using words?

There's one for the books.

I know this: First, I smelled flowers. Cade and Julia drifted toward me, down the trash-strewn and swirling corridor, followed by two shadow puppets. Maybe they were just the shadows of my own scattered atoms. The flower smell got thicker, almost sickening. I looked up and saw the outline of a horse lying on its side, suspended in the mesh net of chain-link overhead.

Here I come, Caballito!

One hundred sideways miles, Finn, and *splat!*

Was it a horse?

Everything waved lazily, the fluttering fingers of sea anemones fanned by back-and-forth warm-water currents.

It was all so beautiful, and in a moment none of it had a name.

If you could feel every atom in your body simultaneously release its grip on its neighbors, expand outward so that each particle becomes a new center in the universe, it would feel exactly like this.

Twenty miles per second, twenty miles per second.

GOING HOME

Later, when I came back together, Julia told me that I had blanked out for about eighty-four-thousand miles—seventy minutes or so.

It was a long and quiet trip.

Somehow I'd ended up on my back, because I found myself staring straight up at all the junk floating in the sky.

Here is another thing about my seizures: Coming back hurts. It hurts a hell of a lot.

As usual, I was very mad.

Look: I lay there, eyes fixed open on the net above me, wondering what it was, marveling at the beautiful honeycomb pattern of narrow lines. It looked like I was staring into the compound lens on the eye of an insect. The sideways horse no longer floated above me—it could not have been there in the first place—but I still didn't have words for the things I saw suspended in the air beneath the third tier.

Words come back so slowly. It is always like that.

Julia and Cade kneeled over me. Cade pressed something soft against the side of my head. It stung.

"Get the fuck off me," I said.

I was never very nice at times like this.

Laika had curled up between my hand and my hip, waiting for me to come back, like she always did when I blanked out.

Laika was a very patient dog.

"Where the fuck did you go?" I said.

Cade shook his head. "Where did *you* go? There's no signal in here. I tried to call your dad."

"Stupid. Don't do that."

Cade Hernandez shrugged. "Doesn't matter, dude. No signal."

"Uh."

I stared and stared. Desk. Chair. Pants. Paper.

Two shadow puppets: The boy on my baseball team and my girlfriend.

Cade Hernandez. Left-handed pitcher.

Julia Bishop.

Twenty miles.

Twenty miles.

Everything hurt so much. My head pounded, and all down my spine it felt as though my bones had been churned to broken shards of glass.

I said, "I'm okay."

:|:

Slowly, I became aware that I had legs, feet, hands. They shook, just like you would shiver if you were submerged in icy water, but I knew it wasn't cold.

I wondered if I pissed myself.

I couldn't move my hand to check if my shorts were wet. My

arms were not connected yet. But I was thinly comforted by the foggy memory of having pissed into an old concrete toilet with Cade Hernandez in what looked like a demolished locker room.

Was any of it real?

I stared at Julia. I tried to see if there was something she could tell me with her eyes—if I was okay, or if I'd pissed myself again, or maybe I was lying there with a goddamned hard-on pitching a circus big top in my shorts. I could see Julia Bishop was scared about something.

Cade pressed and pressed his hand against the side of my head.

"You cut your head," he said.

"Fuck that."

I felt my fingers rake through the greasy spines of Laika's fur.

"Is it bad?" I asked.

Cade pulled his fingers away and leaned in closer. He said, "I don't know. You probably need stitches."

I watched a bead of sweat roll downward from Cade's armpit and turn along the curve of his chest. It was Cade's own shirt he used to press against the cut, which was just at the base of my skull behind my right ear. I could tell it was Cade's shirt; I could smell his atoms on it.

"No fucking way am I going to get stitches," I said.

I swore an awful lot after seizures.

I was always so rebellious whenever I came back from my trips. Nobody likes coming back from vacation, right? But I didn't want my father to find out, which is what would happen if I ended up in some emergency room getting my head sewn shut.

Then I said, "Where the fuck are we, Cade?"

Cade Hernandez turned away from me. I could hear him spit a big stream of tobacco juice down onto the dirty concrete.

Splat!

I shivered and shivered.

After a seizure, I usually need to sleep for twelve hours or so, just to give my atoms a chance to settle in and hold hands again like good neighbors.

It wasn't going to happen this time.

Cade examined the cut on my head one more time. He said, "It looks like it stopped bleeding."

"Sorry about your shirt."

"No worries," Cade said. He winked at me.

Cade Hernandez stood up and then kicked his way through the garbage on the floor, down the corridor toward the toilets.

"Toilet paper," Cade said. "Got to find stuff to use for toilet paper. Pooing without toilet paper is fucking ridiculous."

Cade Hernandez was gone for about fifteen minutes—eighteen-thousand miles.

And we heard him scream.

Clearly, it was a case of Cade being Cade.

By the time he came back, Julia had helped me sit up with my back propped against a cell door. I was groggy.

"It sounded like you were dying in there," I said.

"Dude, it was like having twins. Ridiculous."

That was Cade Hernandez.

We had to get back to Burnt Mill Creek. Cade was scheduled to work that night at Flat Face Pizza.

• • •

The walk back was slow and difficult for me, but I wouldn't say anything about it to Cade and Julia.

We had torn a square of fabric out of Cade's T-shirt, and I kept my hand pressed against it until the blood dried and the cloth bandage stuck to my head. It was going to be a real bitch getting that thing off.

Before we left, Cade Hernandez threw what was left of his bloody shirt down in the trash at Aberdeen Lake State Penitentiary. Who wants to wear a shirt soaked in some other kid's blood?

I offered to give him my own T-shirt, but he said no because he couldn't think up anything new to name my emoticon scar.

:|:

I conceded that two names in one day would be expecting a little too much, even from a left-handed artistic genius like Cade Hernandez.

He let Julia and me sit together in the backseat for the ride home to Burnt Mill Creek, and told me I should take a shower at his house so my mom and dad wouldn't—in his words—think I looked like such a fucking bloody mess.

"Thanks, Cade," I said. "Maybe I *will* hang out with you at Flat Face tonight."

I didn't want to go home.

I thought I'd be able to sleep in the car, but all the words that had come back swirled with nervous worry inside me. Everything was changing; I was afraid to make the wrong decision about choices in the miles ahead of me. It was like Cade Hernandez's roller-coaster waiting line: Here I was at the front, uncertain about whether or not I'd get on board. I leaned my head against Julia Bishop's perfect shoulder.

As we wound south through the canyon toward Julia's house, the sun dipped down and the shadows of the mountains stretched their cloaks across the snaking roadway.

And Julia Bishop said this: "I am not going back to school next month."

"What?"

Cade said, "Are you dropping out?"

She said, "I'm going back home."

"Yeah," Cade answered, "it's about four miles that way."

"What?" I said again.

"I didn't know when to tell you," Julia said. "My parents want me to come home. Back to Chicago."

If I was ever the kind of guy who punched things, I would have put my fist through something—anything—maybe Cade's window. But I'm not the kind of guy who punches things. I'm the kind of guy who sucks all his shitty life inside his personal black hole and pretends everything is perfectly fine.

:|:

Twenty miles.

Twenty miles.

I wanted to say something, but I was afraid my voice would crack like a little kid who just had his milk money swiped by some asshole like Blake Grunwald.

Twenty miles.

And I asked her, "What do *you* want to do?"

And it wasn't me, it was Julia Bishop, who began to cry. She leaned her forehead against the side window. She squeezed my hand in her lap.

"I don't know, Finn. I miss my mom and dad. My home."

I said, "Oh."

There's no balancing shit like that. Part of me knew what was right for Julia. Part of me allowed myself to feel cheated, like I was being robbed again—and look out, kid, here comes another fucking falling horse.

Julia Bishop said, "I have to leave Tuesday."

And Cade Hernandez told us, "What a pair of fucking downers you two are."

PART 3

THE PLANET OF HUMANS AND DOGS

THE SLOWPOKE MOON

The planet of humans and dogs spins and sails, spins and sails. There is nothing I can do about it. Things keep moving. The knackery never shuts down.

Julia Bishop left Burnt Mill Creek.

Laika and I crossed the dry creekbed of San Francisquito Canyon to say good-bye to her on the morning her aunt and uncle drove Julia to the airport in Los Angeles.

"You look nice," I said when she appeared, dreamy and floating like she always seemed, framed within the front door.

"Thank you," Julia said. "I don't think you've ever told me that before."

"I'm sorry for not saying it sooner than now."

My voice cracked. I felt terrible.

Then I said, "Julia Bishop, you are without a doubt the most beautiful girl I have ever seen in the eleven billion miles of my life, and will ever see, no matter how many billions of miles I have to go before the knackery takes me back too."

Julia smiled and looked down at my feet. I was wearing the socks with the sharks on them.

"I have to leave in twenty minutes," she said.

I calculated the distance.

"Want to take a walk for, like, twenty-four-thousand miles or so?"

Julia sighed. "What am I going to do without you, Finn?"

"How can I answer that? I won't be able to ever know what you are going to do without me, Julia, because we are going in different directions."

She held my hand. We walked through the rock garden where we sat together on the night of the perigee moon, and out into the canyon bed as the sun peeked over the rim.

Laika, no doubt sensing something was about to die, stayed at my feet.

On summer mornings at sunup, San Francisquito Canyon is one of the most perfect places on the planet of humans and dogs.

Look: In my father's novel, *The Lazarus Door*, incomers named Earth the planet of humans and dogs because they liked keeping dogs as pets, but they liked human beings as entrees.

"I wish we could go twenty-four thousand miles away," I said.

"Where would that be?"

"One-tenth the distance to the slowpoke moon."

"Probably not a good idea if we plan on breathing and stuff."

"Probably not."

Julia sighed. "Finn, we'll still be—"

She didn't know what to say.

"We will still *be*, Julia."

Across the creek from Julia's house, where the old washed-out road lay in crumbled chunks, stood a concrete abutment that once served as an overpass to the floodwaters of winter and spring.

"This canyon is nothing but a knackery, and now it is pulling us apart too. It never shuts down, does it?"

"What can I say, Finn? It's time for me to go home."

We kissed. I held Julia's face in my hands and wiped the wet at the corners of her eyes with my thumbs.

I said, "In books—sometimes the corny ones—it's always love conquers all, and waiting faithfully forever, but that kind of stuff is stupid when you know you're just going to have to go on and do what you're going to do. Because we will still *be*, won't we? But it would be a good book to be stuck in, I think."

"Everyone likes those kinds of endings, don't they? We'll see each other again. I know we will," Julia said. "We will always remember this. How could you forget me?"

"You need to tell me how it ends—if I can ever get out of the book."

"I don't know the ending. It's something you have to write for yourself. Don't you get it? You have to open the doors. There's nobody else who's going to do it for you."

"Sure thing."

I couldn't say anything else.

We walked back to her house.

I thought I would cry; I was afraid I'd act like a baby in front of Julia and her family, but in the end I held it in perfectly and walked back home and shut myself inside my room.

I was alone again.

:|:

• • •

Look: The incomers—the *real* aliens, not me—in my father's book had the ability to produce vibrational waves that targeted a specific region inside the brains of their human victims. This part of the brain, called Wernicke's arca, is the part that "hears" and decodes language. When it gets stimulated, there is no difference between actually hearing language and only *imagining* you're hearing it, which is why so many starry-eyed religious human beings believed the fallen angel–cannibal aliens were actually messengers from God, as opposed to hungry freeloaders.

Imagine that.

It's a very long book. It also made some people insane with anger.

I mean, what if messengers from God actually *did* want to eat you? Most people would be okay with that; I mean, those famished angels being sent from God and all.

So when the incomers stimulated all those Wernicke's areas, people heard all sorts of nutty things and assumed it was the actual Voice of God delivering absurd orders that eventually got recorded as unarguable law in holy books like the Bible—things like: *Don't wear clothes made from more than one kind of fabric*, and *If a man has sex with a woman during her period, they must be quarantined from the people until you burn a turtledove or a pigeon*, and *If you are wounded in the testicles, your penis should be cut off*.

That last one was terrifying to me.

I also wondered how—or why—you would set a poor bird on fire.

But my favorite message from God in Dad's science fiction novel was this: *Lie down and let me eat you.*

Amen.

Everyone knew something was wrong with me. When Julia went home to Chicago, I stopped trying to fool people with my pretense of being okay.

:|:

I was filled with a winter storm of sorrow and rage, and I needed someone to blame.

After she left, I stayed in my room for about four million miles—two days—with the shades drawn and my phone turned off. I didn't want to see anything; didn't want to talk to anybody. I'd even listen at the door to make sure I could sneak out of my room to take a piss and drink some faucet water once in a while and not have to look at anyone else in my family. I'd pretend to be asleep whenever Mom called up the stairs, telling me to come to dinner.

I was pathetic.

But my misery wasn't a secret to anyone; there was no mystery to be solved at all. The epileptic boy had a broken heart, and it was no big deal to anyone else on the planet of humans and dogs.

At least, not until Dad got tired of my behavior.

On Thursday morning at eleven o'clock, he came into my room.

Hello, gasoline! said Mr. Lit Match.

I was still in bed, a mess. I hadn't showered or put on clean clothes in the millions of miles since I said good-bye to Julia Bishop.

Dad went straight to my window, pulled the blinds back, and opened it.

It was like I'd been unearthed from a coal mine after being trapped for days and days.

"It stinks in here."

There was a definite edge to my father's voice.

"Sorry."

Dad put his hand on my shoulder and shook me.

"You need to get up, Finn. I'm not going to let you stay in here like this any longer. Cade's waiting downstairs, and I exhausted all possible topics of conversation with him back when he was about twelve years old."

Cade Hernandez and I were supposed to leave for our college trip on Friday, the next day. That was the plan.

Not feeling any particular need to be nice to anyone, I said, "Why do you hate him?"

Dad said, "Because he is exactly everything I do not want you to be."

Then he pulled the covers off me. The only thing I had on was a pair of briefs—the free ones we got from Governor Altvatter after Cade Hernandez fixed Burnt Mill Creek High School's BEST Test scores.

We were the smartest junior class in the galaxy!

Cade Hernandez was a god, and I owed him my underwear.

I sat up and hung my feet over the edge of the upper bunk.

"Oh. What *do* you want me to be, Dad? Why don't you just map it out for everyone to see in your next book, and that will be me?"

I caught my dad's eyes. He looked like I'd punched him. It was the meanest thing I'd ever said to my father in my life, but I wasn't about to stop myself from going a step farther. I told him this: "Why don't you leave me the fuck alone?"

It felt like I'd been holding in twelve billion gallons behind the sutures of my Lazarus Door scar. It was time to set them free.

I hadn't noticed Tracy—Mom—was standing in the doorway, listening to us. She carried a tray with breakfast for me.

She said, "You should be ashamed of yourself, Finn."

I was.

Dad had a sickened expression, as though he'd finally lost what he couldn't stand to lose. He went to my door and told Mom to go, that he wanted to talk to me alone. Then he shut my door.

I already knew I'd gone too far; I'd caused a flood and I was caught in it, drowning. Finn Easton's self-taught disaster.

Twenty miles.

Twenty miles.

"Sorry I said that."

"You made your mother cry."

I caught myself before my fourteen-billion-year-old teenage atoms let my mouth say something horrible—that Tracy wasn't my *real* mom, even though she was the only mom I remembered.

"She shouldn't have been standing there. I just want to be left alone."

"Well, that's not going to happen."

I planted my elbows on my knees and propped my chin in my hands as I stared down at my feet dangling above the floor.

My dad took a cautious step toward me. I wasn't looking at him; I could sense him moving closer.

100 SIDEWAYS MILES

He said, "Come on, son, I know exactly how it feels—"

Twenty miles.

Twenty miles.

Dad turned toward the door.

"Okay, Finn. I'll leave you alone. I'll let Cade know the Dunston trip is off."

"Don't tell him that. Maybe I just need to go away or something. Give you a break from me."

"Your mom and I don't really think it would be a good time for you to go, Finn."

"You and Mom can't do anything about what happened to me. I'm tired of being the broken little kid, the fucking epileptic. I'm tired of the way you and Mom and everyone else look at me, like the slightest little fucking wind is going to break me in half again."

"You're broken right now, Finn."

"And your point is *what*? That I'm never going to be able to stand on my own? That I'm going to have to wait and see what kind of ending Easton Michaels dreams up for poor Finn?"

"No."

My father sighed and shook his head.

"Look: I'm sorry for what I said to you, and how I acted. I—I'm just sad about the way things turned out for me. But if you make me stay home now, it would be the worst thing you ever did to me. Sorry. I'll straighten up, Dad."

I felt like shit, and I wanted him to leave before the dam broke.

:|:

ANDREW SMITH

Look: You're allowed to do that at some point when you're a teenager, right? I mean have a meltdown on your parents. Everyone I knew did those things; it just hadn't happened to the epileptic boy until Julia Bishop went away.

We stowed all our gear for the trip inside the camper shell on Cade's truck. On Friday morning, I said my awkward and muted good-byes to Dad and Mom and Nadia, Laika, too. I knew I had been bad, and I had passed off my own personal shit onto my family, but I was a teenager, stubborn, and I wasn't about to give in and blubber my apologies to them, especially not in front of Cade Hernandez.

So Dad was uncharacteristically quiet. He didn't say all those things I'd come to expect: about keeping my phone charged, about using my credit card, about not drinking, about letting him know what I thought about the school, checking in every day, and *making sure Cade Hernandez called him if his little epileptic boy blanked out.*

Seventeen years is almost eleven billion miles traveled together. That's a long enough trip to get to know these things even if they go unspoken.

I guess that's a sign of growing up: When your dad shuts up but you can hear him anyway. Maybe he was the incomer instead of me. Maybe he was fucking with my Wernicke's area.

That day, Cade Hernandez and I crossed the line into Arizona.

The epileptic boy had finally broken out of the prison of California.

THE BERLIN WALL

I said, "I have never been out of the state of California in my life."

"It's about fucking time you said something."

I had been silent and moping for hours, glancing down from time to time in nervousness at the screen on my phone. Dad checked in with three text messages before we'd crossed the Colorado River. After the third, I sent him this: *Everything is okay.*

:|:

And Julia and I had been texting too. I wanted to hear her voice so bad, it was making me crazy, but I was afraid, and I didn't want to talk to her in front of Cade.

Her last message to me was this: *I miss you so much. I love you.*

"I guess I was waiting till after we got to Arizona to say anything."

"That's the dumbest conversational plan I have ever heard in my life."

"You're probably right."

Cade Hernandez spit tobacco into an old plastic water bottle.

Then he nodded and reached across the center console and poked my back with his pointer finger.

"Well, I'm glad the dam finally broke."

Neither of us was wearing a shirt.

And Cade said, "Dude with four balls popping a boner 'cause he's in Arizona."

"Uh, I don't think I would like to have four balls, Cade."

:|:

"Yeah," he said, "a guy would probably never get to sleep."

"Hard enough to sleep with just two," I said.

Cade spit again. "You know what Oklahoma used to be called?"

I had no idea what he was talking about.

"What?"

"Indian Territory."

"Oh."

"K-L-A-H-O-M-A," Cade sang.

"And that's the dumbest thing anyone has said to me in, like, my entire postlingual life, Cade."

"I didn't say it, bitch. I sang it."

Ever since we'd left Burnt Mill Creek, Cade Hernandez must have been calculating some method for successfully extracting an "Oh" from me, and when it finally happened he musically pounced.

Cade laughed and patted the dashboard. Then he held up his right hand and extended his finger toward the steering wheel; kind of like the way a kid might pretend to be holding a gun.

"Go west," Cade said, pointing past the steering wheel.

"Huh?"

I glanced out Cade's side window. I didn't know if he meant we had missed some turn we were supposed to take. But there were no turns here; only undulating straight highway and desert.

"No. It's the map of Oklahoma. It's shaped like a hand with a finger pointing west."

"Are we done talking about Oklahoma yet, Cade?"

"I think I've used up all my material." Then he braced his knee against the steering wheel, pointed his left hand somewhere into the empty space in front of the dashboard air vent, and said, "I guess we're about here."

"You are a human map of the United States," I said.

"Who drives with his knee," Cade added.

My phone tickled in my pocket: Dad and the nonstop status checking via text message. I squirmed in my seat and tweezered my fingers into the pocket of my shorts.

"My dad's texting again," I said.

"Let me see that."

I glanced at my screen just to be certain it really was Dad texting me. No kid wants his best friend to see text messages from a girl who'd broken his heart.

Cade read my father's check-in message, shook his head, then tossed my phone out his window, into the Arizona afternoon.

"Hey! What the fuck?"

"That's exactly why I left mine at home in my bedroom. Your dad is going to drive us crazy. He needs to let you go, dude."

"You left your phone back home?" I was horrified at the thought of not having a single cell phone between the two of us.

Cade added, "Whatever. That's why you have insurance. Tell them a crazy guy threw it out your car window. You can get a new one when we go back home."

"What if something happens?"

I was mad.

Cade shrugged. "Something *will* happen. You don't want to miss it just because you have a cell phone jammed up your ass."

Cade Hernandez and I slept in a forty-five-dollar-a-night motel room somewhere east of Gallup, New Mexico, that smelled like cigarettes and Comet cleanser.

There was a phone with a *dial* in the room. It had a cord, too. I wondered if I would actually have the nerve to call my dad with it in the morning and confess I'd "lost" my cell phone. If I didn't check in soon, I was certain Dad would be notifying the FBI or Homeland Security, or whatever agency is actually in charge of apprehending interstate fugitive epileptic kids who probably came from some other planet.

The motel was called E-Z Rest.

It was the first time I had ever stayed in a motel room.

Imagine that.

And although I never actually remembered the particular details of the months and months I'd spent in a hospital after that dead horse fell a hundred sideways miles and crushed my life, staying in the E-Z Rest brought something back to me that I couldn't exactly express in words. I felt the numb isolation of those days when I was just a little motherless kid, emptied of words, waiting to come through my door and be born.

The man working at the front desk of the E-Z Rest wore a

plastic name badge that said MARTIN pinned to his stained blue polo shirt.

Cade Hernandez said this to him: "We need a room for the night, but we are not gay."

Martin looked at Cade, then me, then back at Cade again, without answering.

So Cade continued. "In fact, Finn here is actually a virgin. Can you believe it? I know, right? What guy Finn's age is still a virgin?"

Martin, unimpressed, said, "It's forty-five dollars. As long as you don't steal the towels, I don't really give a shit what the two of you do in there. I need a credit card and a driver's license."

So we checked in to the E-Z Rest.

"Sometimes I really hate your guts, Cade Hernandez," I said.

After I inserted the key card to unlock the door to room 211, which was where Martin had put us for the night, the first thing I noticed was the room had only one enormous, king-size bed. Martin apparently did not appreciate Cade Hernandez's energy level.

"Uh," Cade said. "Remember, as long as we don't steal the towels, everything else we do is okay with the management."

"Um."

Cade shrugged. "I'll go fix it with Martin downstairs. Get him to switch to a double room."

"I think you should leave him alone. He'll probably throw us out. It's late, and I'm tired."

"I have a cooler full of beer in the truck. Let's get drunk."

I thought about it, then nodded.

"You go get the beer while I construct the Berlin Wall."

Look: The Berlin Wall is this: It is every available pillow and sofa cushion in the room, all lined up directly down the center of the king-size bed where Cade Hernandez and I were going to spend the night. I believe the construction of such barriers is instinctive—like dam building among beavers—when it comes to teenage boys sleeping together in the same bed.

As I put the final touches on the East–West blockade, Cade thumped his way through the door bracing a heavy, sloshing cooler against his knees, and said, "Mr. Gorbachev, tear down this wall!"

Ridiculous.

"Why do I have to live in *East* Berlin?" Cade whined.

We were drunk. To be honest, Cade was drunker. I only managed to finish two beers. The remote control didn't work, so Cade left the television tuned to a sports channel with the sound turned down. The Dodgers were playing a home game, and Cade and I were lying on the bed, drunk, in our underwear.

I had to think for a moment about the location of the highway, which direction the E-Z Rest faced, but Cade was right: He was walled off in East Berlin.

"Be grateful you have electricity and beer, comrade. Germany has no plans for reunification before sunrise." I turned over and shut off the nightstand lamp on my side of the bed. "I'm going to sleep. Good night."

"I'm not tired yet." Cade opened another beer. Then he said, "I'm going to stay up and read awhile."

That was ridiculous. Cade Hernandez reading.

"Yeah. Right."

"Little Bitch."

"You're just jealous because I have a bullfighter name and you don't."

I rolled over and shut my eyes.

"My bullfighter name is Cinco Dólares. Duh."

But as I lay there, something remarkable happened. I heard the sound of Cade Hernandez actually opening a book, thumbing through pages. Despite the heavy musk of cigarettes, sweat, cleanser, and beer in our room, I could actually *smell* the sweet paper scent of a book.

I fought the impulse to look at him, telling myself, *Do not open your eyes and look at what Cade Hernandez is reading. You know it's going to be porn or something awful and embarrassing.*

But it was too much for me to take. I had to look.

When I sat up and peered over our wall, I said, "You have got to be fucking kidding me, Cade."

Cade Hernandez was reading—in the middle of—*The Lazarus Door* by Easton Michaels, my dad.

It was awful and embarrassing.

"Yeah, I know. Ridiculous, huh? Am I the only person in the world who hasn't read this thing yet?"

"Uh."

"I started it a couple days ago, after you quit talking to everyone."

Cade took a swig of beer and continued. "When you think about it, it's kind of pathetic—I realized I don't have any real friends except for you and Julia and Monica Fassbinder, and I got so bored 'cause there was nobody to talk to and no one for me to hang out with this week, so I decided to actually *read a fucking book*."

He turned the page. "So don't bother me. And if you're going to stay up and stare at me while I read a book, you should be quiet and have another beer, Little Bitch."

"Okay, Cinco Dólares."

My head was spinning.

Cade reached down into the ice chest he'd wedged between his side of the bed and the wall. He pulled up a dripping brown bottle of beer.

"Here," he said.

I sat cross-legged in West Berlin and drank.

"Dude," Cade said, "you're in this book."

"I know."

"Do you eat anyone?"

"No."

"Do you get killed?"

"It's not really me," I said. "My dad just named the kid Finn."

"And the incomers just happen to have different-colored eyes and that same thing on their backs as you."

:|:

Cade peered over the top of the Berlin Wall. Unblinking. Staring at the heterochromatic alien boy in the bed next to him, craning his neck to see my naked back.

"If I wake up in the middle of the night and you're chewing on my thigh, I'm going to be pissed."

"Don't fuck with me, Cade."

I turned on my light.

"There's a hell of a lot of sex in this book."

"I know. I've read it. You're only halfway through. Just wait."

"It's kind of creepy—thinking about your dad thinking about sex."

"Then don't think about it."

"You got to wonder about a guy who thinks up a story about angels who eat people after they have sex with them, and then puts his *own kid* in the book."

"It's not me, dumbshit. It's just a story. Fiction."

Cade said, "But I never knew your dad thinks up shit like this. He is seriously fucked up."

I sighed. "Everyone says that to me. It's just a book, okay. He's a writer; he makes shit up. People take it way too serious. There've even been some wackos who said they wanted to kill him for writing that book."

"I thought about killing the fucker who wrote our calculus book."

I nodded. "Yeah. So did I."

"That asshole probably never thinks about sex."

"Calculus is as effective a deterrent to sex as castration."

Cade nodded thoughtfully. "You got an A in it. Virgin."

"Uh. So did you, Cade."

Cade took another drink and shrugged. "Still, if I was all into the Bible and going to church and shit, I'd probably be pissed off at your dad too. He's got balls to fuck around with making fun of angels and God and shit. People go to war over that shit."

"Whatever."

I lay down and stared up at the smoke stains on the cottage-cheese ceiling.

"Well, I can't wait to see what happens to you in the book."

"It's not me."

"Do you at least get *laid*?"

"Shut up."

"Did you ever get pissed off at him for putting shit about you in the book?"

Twenty miles.

Twenty miles.

I said, "Yes."

TRUE GRITS

In a motel room east of Gallup, New Mexico, as we lay separated by the Berlin Wall that cut lengthwise down our king-size bed, I told Cade Hernandez the story of *The Boy in the Book*—the shadow play Julia Bishop imagined for me on the night of my seventeenth birthday. Despite all his assumptions about what may have gone on sexually between Julia and me that night, it was the first time I'd ever said anything about it to my best friend.

Cade said, "Your dad was the monster."

"I think it was a tiger."

"Dude. She's, like, magic or something, for knowing that shit about you."

"I know."

In the morning, I used the cord-and-dial telephone in our motel room to call my father. I felt awkward and guilty about avoiding him, as though every sorrow in my universe had spilled out of his pen, and that he was to blame for everything.

But it was Saturday, after all—our usual morning to have coffee together—and I knew I'd have to get it over with and talk to Dad sooner rather than later.

Cade Hernandez, accomplished sleeper that he was, snored throughout the entire conversation, his face buried beneath a portion of the wall, a somnambulist's unfinished escape tunnel out of the Soviet sector on our king-size bed.

I told Dad I'd lost my phone in Arizona; that it must have fallen out of my pocket. The story was so close to actually being the truth that I did not feel like a liar for saying it. Still, Dad sounded especially doubtful when I added that Cade had forgotten his phone back home in Burnt Mill Creek.

So there was no way for Dad to get hold of us.

Teenagers without cell phones: Imagine that.

I had to promise I would call home later that night from wherever Cade and I got a room. We had a nine-hour drive ahead of us to northern Oklahoma and Dunston University. The school's enrollment fair was set to open the next day, on Sunday.

When I hung up, I leaned across the Berlin Wall to see if Cade was still asleep. I considered phoning Julia, but only until Cade Hernandez's muffled voice rose like hot sewer gas from beneath a sofa cushion: "Get the fuck away from me."

"You told me to wake you up at six. It's six thirty. That's, like, thirty-six thousand miles past six."

"Stop it," Cade moaned. "I fucking hate math. I fucking hate everything when I'm hungover. Please get me some water, dude. Please. I stayed up too late finishing that goddamned book."

Apparently, my dad's novel was not the only thing Cade Hernandez finished after I fell asleep. Empty beer bottles lay scattered all over East Berlin.

I went to the bathroom and ran cold water into a motel glass I unwrapped from a crinkled wax-paper bag.

"Here."

Cade, hair crazy and eyes glazed, sat up from behind the Wall and gulped all the water, spilling at least a third of it down his chest and onto his lap.

I took the glass and refilled it.

Cade said, "And how the hell could he end it like that? He can't just leave you there—alone—and with all those fucking doors opening everywhere. It gave me fucking nightmares. I need to know what's going to happen next."

"Look: two things. First, it is *not me*. Second, you're supposed to figure it out for yourself."

"Horseshit. Make him write another book."

"I can't. He won't. So deal with it."

"When we go back home, I'm going to give him an aneurysm for fucking with my head like that."

"Uh."

Cade combed his fingers through his wild hair. "Okay. I'll tell him if he writes another book, I'll let him put me in it. He can even kill me if he wants."

"That's bound to work, Cade."

I made a third trip to the bathroom sink to get my friend more water.

• • •

The First words of my father's novel are these:

> My dear child: When these immigrants arrive, they do not come as passengers carried in the bellies of mechanical whales.

> There are no lights, no music of thunder.

> One of the first arrivals lands in the calm center of an eye on a black Oregon lingcod lying curled, an orphaned parenthesis atop a pillow of crushed ice at a stall rented by a fishmonger named Mr. Otani.

> The place smells of lemon and damp unfinished wood.

Everything served for breakfast at La Posada Restaurant came with a choice of hash browns or grits.

"What's *grits*?" Cade asked.

After we checked out of the E-Z Rest, Cade and I stopped for breakfast before settling in to the final leg of our long drive.

"They're made from hominy," I explained.

"What's that?"

"It's kind of—I don't really know. Gigantic white corn or something."

"Does it taste like corn?"

"Not really."

Cade Hernandez squinted and leered at me from the corner of his eye.

"How come you know so much about grits and hominy and shit like that?"

"Grits taste exactly like human meat."

Cade nodded. "I thought that must be it."

We both ate our first-ever grits with breakfast at La Posada. Our waitress, a short woman with ample breasts whose name was Florencia, according to the bright sombrero-shaped badge pinned to her pink apron, told us the way her husband preferred to eat his grits was with salt, butter, and a few drops of hot sauce.

The grits tasted very good.

Cade said, "If this is what human meat tastes like, it's no wonder you fuckers all came through those doors after us."

"Told you so."

"Can you do that thing?"

"What thing?"

"You know—like the incomers do in the book—stimulate the Wiener area in my brain so I hear you telling me something you want me to do."

"I think your entire brain is a Wiener area."

"That kind of gives me a boner."

"Can you hear me telling you to shut the fuck up?"

Cade Hernandez smiled and nodded. "Yep."

Look: It can be proved by observing the motion of objects in the universe that wherever you are is the precise center.

No matter how fast you move, you will never get anywhere if that's the case.

That afternoon, Cade Hernandez and I traversed the desolate panhandle of Texas and crossed over the line into Oklahoma.

ANDREW SMITH

It felt so distant from San Francisquito Canyon and home. And this was nothing—a moment of motion through space— but I wondered at all that distance above and below me, how big this universe might actually be; how fast it all moved.

Eighty miles away from Dunston—four seconds in Earth time—the first bullet-gray, thumb-size drops of rain plunked down all over the blacktop and Cade's truck, pelting us with a staccato machine-gun peppering—*thak! thak! thak!*

Within a few minutes, the curtains of rain became so heavy and dark, we could not see more than ten feet ahead of us on the highway.

"It's a fucking flood," Cade said.

To be more accurate, Cade Hernandez practically shouted. The roar of the rain was deafening.

I did not know whether it was an actual flood, but I had never seen rain as heavy as what fell on us in Oklahoma that day. Comparing the rainstorms I'd seen in California with what we drove through that August afternoon was like comparing a parakeet's birdbath with the twelve-billion-gallon St. Francis Reservoir.

The highway transformed into a slate-colored river, spiked and prickled by relentless fat globules of rain. Cade slowed the truck, or perhaps, I thought, the rain pushed so hard against us that surface gravity doubled on the planet of humans and dogs.

"This is ridiculous," I said.

"I should pull over, but I can't tell where *over* is."

In fact, the road and all markings on it had been swallowed up beneath the rising black waters. Cade navigated by aiming his steering wheel toward two pinpoints of red—the taillights on whatever car was driving ahead of us. All around, everything else blended into an indistinguishable, borderless cascade of blurring gray streaks.

"Holy shit!" Cade swerved and braked.

An eighteen-wheel tractor-trailer rig—a whale in the rain—passed on our left, going more than double our speed. It sprayed a blinding sheet of rainwater that washed over Cade's windshield and nearly swept us from the road.

"Maybe we should stop and wait it out," I said.

But when the truck passed the next car ahead of us, covering it with spray, the two little red lights we followed veered sharply to the right and then vanished—winked out—completely.

"Did you see that?" Cade said.

He slowed his pickup to a stop and inched over to what I assumed was the shoulder of the highway.

"That car up there went off the road," Cade said.

"I lost sight of it after that truck passed him," I said.

"Dude."

So we sat there for a moment, swallowed in an Oklahoma fire-hose rainstorm.

Twenty miles.

Twenty miles.

The rain roared, swirling like angry black bees in the wild wind. I imagined the force of it crumpling the metal husk of Cade Hernandez's pickup.

"Is this normal for Oklahoma?" I said. "Because if it is . . . well, shit."

Cade shook his head and shrugged. "Fuck if I know."

He snapped his can of tobacco and packed a black wad behind his lower lip.

"Let's wait till this shit lets up," I said.

"If we have to, we can sleep in the back. We have plenty of beer and food."

That was true. We'd also brought along our sleeping bags. Neither one of us was interested in pressing on to Dunston now that we had successfully come to a complete stop.

"Don't you think we should go up there and see if the people in that other car are okay?" I asked.

Cade Hernandez spit a brown glob into his spittoon bottle.

"I was hoping you wouldn't ask that," he said, "but I guess there's nothing else we can do. If you want to wait in the car, I can go look. No sense in both of us ending up half-drowned."

Cade Hernandez could be such a hero at times.

Twenty miles.

Twenty miles.

"We'll go together," I said.

The rain hammered and hammered.

THE BOY, THE DOG, AND THE EPILEPTIC

We were drenched before we made it past the front bumper on Cade Hernandez's pickup.

Who would have thought to bring along foul-weather gear?

Cade Hernandez and I wore improbable outfits for rescuers in hurricanes: mesh basketball shorts, sneakers, and baseball raglans—the blue-sleeved undershirts from our Pioneers uniforms—all of which sponged up the rainwater and plastered against our bodies, slogging and sloshing, weighing us down and slowing our pace, as though everything danced hypnotically in an underwater dream.

The only sound came from the gusting winds and spit-warm pregnant rain; there was no traffic at all moving on the highway. We splashed along the side of the road—fifty, one hundred feet ahead of the pickup—and with each step my sneakers drank more and more, growing heavier and heavier until the weight threatened to pull my shoes from my feet.

Cade found fresh tire ruts cutting across the muddy shoulder where the car we'd been following had slid from the highway.

Ahead of us, something black and skeletal seemed to loom up from the middle of the road.

What I saw through the downpour was the metal truss frame on a bridge.

I grabbed Cade's shoulder and pointed. "There's a bridge here."

I wondered if anyone ever jumped from it with elastic lashings wrapped around their ankles.

"They went down the bank," Cade said.

It did not look good. Bridges, because they are usually sensibly planned civil-engineering projects, are only built to go over things— often, things with lots of water in them. And this bridge happened to cross Little Buffalo River, wide and dark, but not what anyone with eyesight would call "little" by a long shot.

Cade and I followed the muddy wheel ruts through the waist-high grass down the slope of the river's embankment. As I might have expected, my shoes came off in the suction of mud and water, and I tramped after my friend in my drooping socks.

The rain never slackened in the least.

Thirty feet from the edge of the highway, we caught sight of the roof of a dark green van through the tangles of buttonbush along the river's shore. The van was nearly submerged, drifting sideways and slowly sinking beneath the rain-boiled surface.

"Hey! Is anyone here? Can you hear me?" Cade shouted to see if maybe whoever was inside the van had managed to get out. But there was no answer. And we could both see that none of the doors on the vehicle were open.

A pale white hand slapped against the darkened glass of the van's rear window.

Look: There are times when you can be faced with a situation that presents no alternatives between *dothis* and *dothat*. And if there was one thing the epileptic kid could do just as effortlessly as blanking out, it was this: I could swim.

Dothis.

At first, Cade Hernandez and I tried to get to the van by working our way through the tangles of brush that walled the shore, but the shrubs grew so thick, and the bank was too steep and soft from the swamping by the storm. Where the van's undercarriage had mown down the brush, spiny branches jutted up like deadly spikes. It was impossible to get to the water.

"Let's go up this way," I said.

I pointed to the bridge above us.

"What the hell are you thinking?" Cade said.

"I'm going to jump from the bridge."

I did not wait for Cade to reply. I scrambled back up the bank to the bridge's abutment. On the way, the sucking mud stole my ruined socks from my feet, and then I squirmed out of my baseball sleeves and tossed the soaked raglan down onto the roadway.

Once I made it far enough out on the bridge, above a point in the river I'd estimated it would be safe to jump into, I considered the ridiculousness of my situation: the circuitous irony of my life—its perfect orbit at twenty miles per second, twenty miles per second. Caballito—the Little Horse—was jumping from a bridge.

Here I come, Mom!

It rained and rained.

The wind swirled and howled.

ANDREW SMITH

I didn't know if Cade had followed me up onto the bridge or not; I wasn't thinking about anything else at all.

Two deep breaths.

Twenty miles.

Twenty miles.

The van sank lower.

And I leapt.

And I hung in the air, descending more slowly than the rain, falling sideways, falling sideways.

The current was strong. The river clenched me in its fist, gritty and brown, much colder than I thought it would be. As soon as I came up to the surface, spitting and gulping air, I spun around to orient myself: There was the van, turning toward me so slowly near the bank, a flashing glimpse of a face and a flattened palm behind the rear window, tilted up in the pyramidal air pocket at the tail of the cabin. The face was like a ghost—sticky atoms refusing to give way and cooperate with the will of the knackery. Marjorie and Mazie caught in the sweeping demolition of William Mulholland's mass-execution device.

Behind me, the black underbelly of the bridge hovered, a monstrous vulture swooping thirty feet overhead.

Cade Hernandez stood atop the steel safety railing, barefoot and shirtless, white as vanilla ice cream, teetering to find a spot in the water where he wouldn't land on me. It wouldn't have happened anyway: The force of the current pushed me backward, dragging my body under the bridge.

I had to swim hard.

I caught a glimpse of midair Cade, a gangly pale missile

diving headfirst through the rain, hands stretched toward the center of the muddy river. And I reached and reached, pulling massive armfuls of the water back along my sides as I kicked through the current.

It felt like I was swimming inside a cement mixer. The basketball shorts I had on dragged like sails, slowing me down, coaxing me away from the van.

Time expanded in every imaginable direction. Twenty miles will always be twenty miles, but seconds in that water exploded into hours, weeks.

The current seemed to cut around me once I wormed my way to the upriver side of the van. The van turned and tilted. I slapped my palm against the roof and yelled, "Hey!"

The windows were all below the surface now, swallowed beneath the brown water.

A knocking answered from inside the van. I saw Cade Hernandez's arms frantically splashing toward me from the center of the river. I held my breath and went under, feeling along the van's side panel until I found the handle of a door.

I pulled as hard as I could. My fingers slipped from the handle, and I realized the door had given only an inch because it was a slider door. The river world was all brown and shadowy forms—a universe of nameless undefined matter below the surface. I pushed the door backward and slipped into the van.

It was a ridiculous scene inside—an underwater recreation of the hovering garbage at Aberdeen Lake State Penitentiary. When I forced the door open, the van's cabin lights came on, illuminating plastic grocery bags that floated and waved like jellyfish, a bundle of celery pirouetting like a compass needle, a yellow box of Triscuit crackers pinned to the ceiling. At the front of the van, a motionless dark shape of a person—someone was belted into the driver's seat. It did not look good; the driver's arms fanned lifeless over the top of the dashboard as though playing an invisible piano.

Then I felt the bottom of a tennis shoe scrape against my ribs.

It was a kid I'd seen pressing his small hand against the back window of the van.

I pulled myself over the third-row seats and got my head up inside the tiny pocket of air in the rear corner. The kid was small and scared, about six or seven years old—maybe just four billion miles or so—with thin buckwheat hair that was plastered down against his ghostly skin. He tried to say something to me, but his jaw shuddered so bad, all he could do was gurgle and moan. And he held up a small dirt-colored dog that kicked its back legs like it was trying to swim free of the boy's arms.

The planet of humans and dogs.

The van slid around and began to tip onto its side.

The pocket of air constricted, and we pressed our mouths and noses up into the fabric on the van's ceiling. It smelled like cigarette smoke. Sticky atoms.

I grabbed onto the collar of the kid's T-shirt.

"You need to hold your breath. I'm taking you out. Okay?"

The kid didn't say anything; only stared at me with dollar-size eyes.

"You ready?"

I tugged and jerked.

The boy, the dog, and the epileptic kid all went under.

Look: I can only imagine what it must have been like to be alive in San Francisquito Canyon the night of William Mulholland's great failure.

Atoms would be scattered.

Marjorie and Mazie Curtis lived in a small cabin built near the power plant, just below the towering dam. When the St. Francis Dam first broke, their mother heard the sound of it and woke the girls' father.

Look: When a dam breaks, it doesn't explode like a bomb. The first thing to happen is a fracture forms. Then twelve billion gallons of water molecules crowd for that initial escape vent, and they tear and chew at the structure until house-size chunks of it tumble down its disintegrating face.

Lillian Curtis's father, who helped build the road to the dam—the same road that I would one day live on—warned the family that living beneath the massive dam was not safe; that they should build their home on the canyon rim. But the Curtis family was determined to live under the St. Francis Dam.

So when she heard the angry noise from the first fracture and the rumbling growl of the water as it grew louder and louder, Lillian Curtis told her husband that she would carry their three-year-old son, Danny, up the face of the canyon.

Three years is less than two billion miles.

Lyman Curtis agreed to take their daughters, Marjorie and Mazie, but he needed to check in at Power Plant No. 1 first. I have never understood why men with regular, difficult jobs can sometimes feel an unexplainable dedication to a company, but my atoms have not been together for so many miles.

Lyman Curtis was a true Edison Company man.

Lillian ran, barefoot and in her nightgown, up the canyon wall, carrying the little boy. The family's dog, whose name was Spot, followed.

They were the only three to survive.

In 1928, lots of people had dogs named Spot. Now, not so much.

Lillian and Danny sat at the top of the canyon and waited until the following morning. Lillian Curtis's feet were so badly cut that she had to tear bandages from her nightgown. She believed she would find Lyman and the girls again, but her husband apparently never came back for the girls.

Marjorie and Mazie's bodies were so covered in mud and oil that they were not easily identified. I don't know exactly where the oil came from, although there are still a few working oil wells not far from the site of William Mulholland's death trap.

The sisters' bodies were kept about ten miles from the dam in a makeshift morgue for victims. Lyman's body was found more than twenty miles away.

Imagine that.

And I saw those little girls in my house the night I blanked out and pissed myself in front of Julia Bishop.

Here is one more thing about my father's book, *The Lazarus Door*: The story is set in 1928, and part of it takes place in San Francisquito Canyon the night of the failure of the St. Francis Dam.

Sometimes—especially those times when I feel as though

I've been trapped inside my father's book—I wonder if I haven't actually been on this Finn trip for many more miles than seventeen years might carry a guy.

Getting out of the van was more difficult than getting into it. The kid scratched and kicked. What would you expect? He was terrified and probably thought I was some alien monster. And the van tipped, shuddering as the flow of the river pushed through the open side door.

I wrapped the boy under my right arm; and he held on so tight, I could feel each one of his little fingernails cutting smiles into the skin on my chest and ribs. The dog squirmed free just as I found the doorway, and when the kid jerked to catch the thing, he brought his knee right up into my balls.

The hurt knocked all the air from my lungs, and I choked, convinced the two of us were about to drown. Somehow, I managed to kick away from the van and raised my face up into rainfall again, blurry eyed, knotted in painful cramps, and coughing so hard, I thought I'd puke.

The boy was nearly drowned. He spit and snotted all over my neck as he tried to gulp air.

And Cade was there, struggling to pull himself over the roof of the van as the current tipped it toward him. The van was rolling onto its side.

Cade gurgled as he fought the river. "Fuck!"

I coughed and kicked, treading water with one arm while trying to keep the kid's face above the surface.

Cade thrashed behind the van. "Are you okay?"

"There's someone else in there. In the driver's seat." I shook my head, hoping Cade would know I didn't think it was worth the risk of him going under for that shadowy body.

But once the kid and I made it around the nose end of the van, the current pulled us into the deep center of the river, away from Cade and the van, carrying us under the bridge. My guts constricted in pain, and my legs burned with acid. I was too weak to swim against the current with the drag of the fighting kid under my arm.

I looked up and saw the black bar of the bridge span pass over us. I couldn't see the van or Cade Hernandez at all. I rolled onto my side so the kid was on top of me, and scissored my legs in an attempt to have the river push us toward the opposite bank.

Twenty miles.

Twenty miles.

It took so long. The muddy river distorted and widened, kept us helpless in the groove of its central channel, pulling and pulling.

"Just relax. You're going to be okay."

I don't know if I said it to myself or to the kid. The boy seemed to soften and calm down. I could not say how far we'd gone, but at a widening bend of the river, I felt us slow in the eddying current along the other shore.

My feet dragged against something solid as we neared the bank, and I attempted to stand, holding the little boy in my aching arms. We fell down three times, and I bashed my shins into the river rocks at the shallow edge. Finally, I could let go of the kid, and he scrambled up through the mud and weeds like a wet cat breaking frantic from a bathtub.

By some miracle, the kid's little dog was there too, shaking and licking at the boy while he puked and puked onto the ground between his hands.

Exhausted, I could barely stand in the waist-deep current, tangled up in my shorts, which had pulled halfway down to my knees. I was scuffed and raked with scratches from the clawing kid, who curled up on his side and hugged his legs in a tight little ball on the shore, shivering and watching me with accusing eyes as though I had done this to him.

And from everywhere came the sweet scent of flowers.

Ridiculous.

What could I do?

Twenty miles.

The drifting set in, the sandstorm of atoms spraying across my field of vision as I pushed myself toward the shore and howled in my head to not let go, not let go, while the river seemed to erase everything below my knees, washing it all away into the nameless rain.

THE DOG HOSPITAL

I woke up in what looked like an alien spacecraft.

To be honest, I had no idea what any of it was—the words were so stubborn about finding their way back to the epileptic's drained lexicon.

A tiny, brilliant sun waved in my eye.

It was some time, thousands and thousands of miles, before *allthis* and *allthat* congealed into something definable: I was lying there naked and covered with a blanket atop a cold examination table at a veterinarian's clinic.

It was ridiculous.

The white-hot pinpoint of sun winked out.

"Cade? Your name is Cade, right? Do you have any idea what happened?"

Of course I could not remember anything at all. And all I could see was a blurry orange chrysanthemum where the pinpoint sun had burned its memory into my eye. But something clicked when the floating voice asked me if my name was Cade.

I remembered two words: Cade Hernandez.

And two more: Wernicke's area.

I did not know what that meant.

Imagine that.

"Where am I?"

The chrysanthemum faded.

"Sorry about the accommodations. You're kind of in a dog hospital, I guess."

Dog.

Hospital.

Plaid.

That's the name of the pattern on the man's shirt.

Green.

Welcome home, words!

And then I was pissed off; I was pissed off about being naked and cold in a hospital for fucking dogs, and for knowing almost nothing else.

I was pissed off about everything, the constriction of my universe down to a dozen or so words, but I didn't exactly know why.

There had to be more words than these; I just couldn't find them.

"You passed out," the man told me. "You must have hit your head. You don't have a concussion, though, and I couldn't find any injury on your scalp. Cade?"

Why was he calling me that? But I couldn't remember if it was my name or not.

Imagine that.

He smiled. He had a kind face, tan and wrinkled around his eyes. He slipped the light-pen into the pocket of his shirt and

ANDREW SMITH

removed his black-framed reading glasses, which hung in front of his chest on a thick cord. The walls of the room were pale yellow, and behind him I saw a glossy poster with a puppy on it—an advertisement for a flea treatment. A stethoscope coiled like a snake inside a slotted Plexiglas wall bracket.

A round stool with a black vinyl cushion sat in the corner of the room.

Everything was wet. I thought I might have pissed myself. I still couldn't remember anything at all that happened before I opened my eyes inside the dog hospital.

I might as well have just been born, or just wormed through a Lazarus Door—one atom at a time.

I asked it again. "Where am I?"

The man frowned and leaned over me, staring directly into my eyes as though he might be able to see the empty shelves behind them.

"Interesting. Heterochromatic eyes. I just told you. You're in my clinic. It's for animals, but the closest ER is sixty miles from here."

Sixty miles.

Three seconds.

He went on, "Do you feel pain anywhere?"

My arms and legs weren't fully connected yet. I shook my head.

He told me his name: Nathan Pauley, Doctor of Veterinary Medicine, and that he and Billy Gruber, who was a deputy from someplace called Coal Hill, found my abandoned truck, left with its motor idling near Little Buffalo Bridge. When they searched around the area for me, they passed a little boy standing with his dog on the side of the highway. That was nearly two miles away from the bridge. The boy and his dog had been pulled from the river, and he led the men to where I'd blanked out with my face in the mud of the shore and the rest of me—my shorts twisted around my left ankle—in the cold water. They identified me because Cade Hernandez's California driver's license—and all Cade's belongings—had been left inside the idling truck.

Of course.

It was supremely ridiculous, but at that moment I finally remembered who I was. And I imagined here I was poised at the perfect doorway to break out of the prison of my father's book. I had become someone else.

Cade Hernandez.

They'd brought me here and had no idea that Cade was still out there.

Naturally, the men would not have guessed there were two of us in Cade Hernandez's truck. The epileptic kid—me, Finn Easton—didn't have a driver's license. And Cade had left his wallet sitting on the dashboard when we took off that morning.

Cade Hernandez and I looked so much alike, we could have been brothers.

So Nathan Pauley and Billy Gruber had solved the mystery of where the naked and half-drowned kid came from.

:|:

"How did I get here?"

"In the backseat of Billy Gruber's Jeep," Pauley said.

Billy Gruber, at that moment, was on his way to Coal Hill with a dog and a six-year-old boy named D. J. Klein, the kid I'd pulled from Little Buffalo River, which was big enough to swallow pretty much whatever it wanted to.

I sat up, dizzy, wrapping the blanket tightly around my waist.

"That was a very brave thing you did," Pauley said. "You're quite a hero."

What happened in the river didn't play clearly in my head.

"Where's Cade?" I said. I had a dim memory of seeing Cade Hernandez swimming in my backyard pool. I had no idea at all where I was—that there was such a place called Oklahoma.

The veterinarian put a hand on my shoulder. "Maybe you should lie back down. Billy's sending an ambulance out from Coal Hill."

"No."

Pauley scrunched his eyebrows together.

Then another word came back, and I said, "I'm an epileptic."

Pauley nodded as though the word filled in every blank answer on the scorecard.

I needed to find Cade. They'd left him at the river. They had no way of knowing there had been anyone else.

And then I remembered being underwater, inside the van, the floating box of Triscuit crackers pinned to the roof.

"What about the car?" I said.

"I followed Billy in it. I brought your truck here. It's out front."

"No. Not that."

The dog doctor thought I was talking about *my* car. I couldn't force the words out right. I felt like I'd explode.

"Fuck this," I said.

I held the blanket around my waist and stood.

"Whoa there." The doctor, who obviously had experience with

horses, raised his open hands as though preparing to catch me.

And I'll admit it: The rush of blood did make me wobble and take hold of the corner of the metal table I'd been lying on, to keep myself from falling down.

Twenty miles.

"My clothes are in the back."

I took two steps toward the examination-room's door. The floor was cold under my feet. Everything felt like refrigerated meat.

"I can get them for you. Really. You need to take it easy, son."

"No."

I pushed past the doctor and opened the door.

And I said it again: "Where the fuck am I?"

Of course I had no way of knowing how to get out of the clinic. I steered myself toward the end of the hallway, imagining the light I saw there came from the sky, the outside world on the planet of humans and dogs.

Nathan Pauley stayed right beside me, trying to talk me out of going outside to Cade's truck, but I wasn't about to listen. He was careful. Nathan Pauley was a head shorter than me, and I felt like I would punch him if he touched me again. Something about waking up cold, wet, and naked in a dog hospital had made me so incompliant and irritated.

"Look," Pauley said, "Billy is tracking down your family in California to call them. Do you live in California? Do you remember how to reach them?"

Too many questions.

"Get the fuck away from me."

I pushed through the door at the end of the hallway and

ANDREW SMITH

came out into the clinic's waiting room. There was a floor-to-ceiling window beside the front door, painted with letters that spelled out the doctor's name and business hours in reverse. It made no sense. Nothing at all made sense to me. And through the window I could see Cade's truck. It had stopped raining, and the clear sky was just at that darkening point as the sun dipped in the west.

And then I felt Nathan Pauley's hand on my shoulder again. He said, "That's an interesting scar you have."

:|:

"Tell me where you came from."

I balled my hand into a fist.

What an idiot he was! He must have somehow put it all together: the epileptic boy with the two-colored eyes and the Lazarus Door mark along his spine. He probably thought if I hadn't blanked out, I would have eaten the little kid I pulled from the river.

Even in the state of Oklahoma—Indian Territory—the boy could not escape the prison of the book.

I pushed the doctor's hand away from me and cocked my fist back, but as angry as I was, I couldn't punch the guy.

"Leave me alone."

I went outside, barefoot and naked inside a dog-hospital blanket. Everything was humid and damp, and whereas I'd been freezing cold inside the examination room, I felt sweat droplets trickling from my armpits by the time I made it to Cade's truck.

Nathan Pauley slowed and stood back, watching me outside the clinic's front door.

And I was only wishing to myself, *Please let the keys be in the truck; please remember how Cade Hernandez taught you to drive; please do not crash; please get the hell out of here.*

He must not have thought I'd actually try to drive off. Nathan Pauley must have assumed I was only going for my clothes, like I told him I was. I guess people in Oklahoma are more reliable and compliant than people from Southern California. But the veterinarian got a troubled and disappointed look on his face when I slid in behind the wheel of Cade's truck and started it up.

He stepped forward, waving, "Hey! Wait! You can't leave! Incomer Boy! Wait!"

A DETOUR IN THE YEAR WE GREW UP

Look: I'll admit I drive like a drunken twelve-year-old.

The truck rattled and jerked. I was so uncoordinated with the clutch; and the blanket wrapped around my legs didn't make driving any easier. So when I came to the exit of the parking lot at the dog hospital, I realized I had no idea where I should go.

Thisway or *thatway*?

I turned right, not because I thought it was the direction that would take me back to the river, back to look for Cade. Although I hoped it was, I turned right because it was easier than pulling across the highway and turning left, and I was naked and wrapped in a flea-infested blanket and pissed off, and I wanted to get the hell away from Nathan Pauley, D.V.M., and the possible return appearance of Deputy Billy Gruber—both of whom probably believed I was a child-eating naked alien named Cade Hernandez.

As it turned out, the easier choice was the correct choice.

About a mile from the veterinarian's clinic, I saw flashing red and blue lights in the rearview mirror.

It was ridiculous.

And it was definitely not what I ever imagined would happen to Finn—the incomer boy, not me—when he found himself alone on the planet of humans and dogs at the end of my father's novel.

One thing that did not happen at the end of my father's book was this: Finn did not find himself naked and driving his best friend's pickup truck while being pursued by some type of emergency vehicle with agonizingly bright headlamps and a flashing red beacon that pulsed so vividly across the flat Oklahoma landscape, the spectacle nearly induced the smell of flowers and another epileptic seizure.

And it wasn't just one vehicle behind me; there were several. I pulled the truck onto the gravel of the shoulder and flipped the rearview mirror away so I wouldn't have to look at all those oncoming lights, which soon passed me and sped off down the highway.

The lights were attached to a fire truck, an ambulance, a wrecker tow truck, and in the rear of the urgency parade, a black-and-white county sheriff's patrol vehicle, which was most likely driven by someone named Billy Gruber.

It was a great relief they weren't pursuing me. I thought they likely were rushing to the place where Cade Hernandez and I had jumped into the Little Buffalo River, and how long ago was that, anyway?

Sitting there, the words and pictures came back to me.

I remembered seeing Cade on the upriver side of the sinking van as the kid and I drifted away in the current, how I'd tried to warn him not to go inside for the shadow person belted into the driver's seat. And I remembered how that little boy scratched and kicked me, and that we ended up so far downriver before I could finally drag myself toward the shore.

Then *poof!* and thousands of miles later, my universe became the dog hospital.

I pulled back onto the road and sped after the parade of official vehicles. The flashing lights led me down the highway, toward the bridge.

I turned off the headlights and parked Cade's truck on the side of the road in what was probably the exact spot where we'd abandoned the vehicle hours—all those empty miles—before. Ahead of me, the bank around the bridge was all awash in hot white spotlights. Two men in coveralls stretched a thick steel cable with a hook from the back of the wrecker down toward the brush at the edge of the river.

Near the footing of the bridge, firefighters lifted a wheeled gurney to slide it inside the open doors on the ambulance. Someone was lying on it. But it wasn't Cade Hernandez on the stretcher; I could clearly see it was an old man.

And as I sat there watching it all, Cade Hernandez, wearing nothing but a pale blue disposable paper jumpsuit, came up around the driver's side of the truck from somewhere in the darkness behind me.

I nearly jumped completely out of my dog-hospital blanket when he slapped the door and said, "Dude. Why did you steal my truck? Are you *naked?*"

"Uh."

I didn't know what to say, but I was so relieved to have found my friend.

Or, he found me.

"Dude. That's ridiculous."

"Cade?"

"What?"

"Are you okay?"

"Dude."

"Let's get the fuck out of here."

"I know."

So, clutching my dog blanket around my hips, I stepped out of the truck and limped awkwardly to the passenger side while Cade slid in behind the wheel.

Then we drove off and left the Little Buffalo River behind us.

"You *are* naked, aren't you?" Cade said.

"I lost my clothes in the river," I explained.

"That kind of gives me a boner, which is ridiculous when all you have on is a tissue-paper jumpsuit."

So there we were, both of us driving through Oklahoma in the nighttime, and both of us essentially naked.

Cade said, "You could probably end up getting shot for driving around naked in Oklahoma."

"Um, okay."

"L-A-H-O-M-A!" Cade sang.

"Uh."

After I explained what I remembered about pulling the boy and his dog from the van, and then waking up in Dr. Nathan Pauley's dog hospital, Cade Hernandez told me this story of what happened to him while we were separated.

"Diving was a big mistake," he began. "Never dive off a thirty-foot-high fucking bridge wearing basketball shorts."

I jumped from the bridge, feet first.

"Because as soon as I hit the water," Cade said, "bam! I was stripped clean out of my shorts. Totally naked, too. They went one way, I went the other. It was ridiculous. Nobody wants to get saved by a naked guy. I'm, like, 'Hello! I'm naked, and I'm here to save you, dude.' It was like popping through a Lazarus Door, only I didn't have wings, and I wasn't very horny."

Cade Hernandez would not let go of that book.

"You pulled someone out?" I said.

Cade reached across me and grabbed a can of chewing tobacco from the glove compartment.

He inhaled with satisfaction after he packed a wad of tobacco behind his lip, then Cade spit into his water bottle.

"That grandpa dude who was strapped in the driver's seat," he said. "It didn't look good. The van was tipping over, and I was pretty sure the guy was dead, but I pulled him out anyway and got him up in the weeds on the other side of the bridge. He wasn't breathing, so I did CPR on him. It was fucking ridiculous. There I was, naked and muddy, making out with some old man I pulled out of a minivan beside what looked like a parking lot at a truck stop. I'm lucky I didn't get arrested for being a naked fucking perv or something. I think half the state of Oklahoma saw me doing it there after I got him out of the water, and I was just, like, what the fuck happened to Finn? And why am I fucking naked and sucking on some old dude's face while a bunch of redneck truckers are standing there on the side of the road watching me? Dude. They took pictures with their cell phones. I'm probably naked on a million fucking websites by now."

Cade spit.

"But you saved the guy's life."

"So, yeah. We are both naked heroes, dude."

"Maybe you should find a spot to pull off so we can get some clothes on."

Cade spit again and said, "And the worst part was, just when the guy was ready to kick in and breathe on his own, the dude puked right into my mouth."

I was horrified and repulsed.

And Cade Hernandez said, "I wanted to punch the fucker so bad after that. If this was California, my life would be ruined. Well, probably your life would. I told everyone my name was Finn Easton, from Burnt Mill Creek, California."

Cade Hernandez had become me, and I had become Cade Hernandez.

"That kind of gives me a boner," I said.

Cade spit. "Dude, you're a fucking idiot."

"The guy at the dog hospital looked in your wallet and saw your license, so he thought I was *you*."

"Hmmm. I bet he saw that I have a couple of those colored condoms in my wallet too. Or, should I say *you* do? I bet dudes in Oklahoma never seen colored condoms."

I shook my head. In his wallet? I would never keep condoms in my wallet. Some guys never learn.

"What does someone else's throwup taste like?"

"It wasn't as bad as you'd think," Cade said.

We put on dry clothes standing beside Cade's truck in an empty camping area at a place called Bernice State Park.

I was very happy to get rid of my dog blanket. It made me itch.

Cade Hernandez simply ripped his way out of his rescue outfit.

"Dude. Paper clothes are ridiculous. Why would anyone invent something as dumb as paper clothes? You can see right through them. The cop who gave me this thing said they use it whenever they arrest naked people, like it's something they do all the time in Oklahoma."

"Someone ought to keep statistics on that," I said.

"Dude. What do you think your dad will do if the cops track you down and tell him they found you naked on the side of a river in Oklahoma doing CPR on some old fucker who puked in your mouth?"

Look: To be honest, the thought had not occurred to me.

I stepped into some clean State of California underwear and pulled on another pair of Burnt Mill Creek Pioneers basketball shorts. Neither of us had brought along a very diverse wardrobe.

"I don't know," I said. "I imagine your mom and dad will have something to say after they hear about how you passed out saving a little boy and woke up naked in a dog hospital too. I think this thing gave me fleas."

I scratched myself.

Cade said, "I guess getting someone else's puke in your mouth is just as bad as getting a strange dog's fleas on your balls."

We spent the night at Bernice State Park stretched out atop our sleeping bags in the mess of Cade's camper shell. There were no other humans visible in the campground; and we'd both had all the interaction with people from Oklahoma we could tolerate for one day.

For some reason, having sleeping bags unrolled and camping

out inside a truck bed—which was smaller than the king-size bed we'd shared at the E-Z Rest motel the night before—canceled out the instinct-driven construction of a Berlin Wall, which was kind of ridiculous, because Cade Hernandez and I were so cramped together inside his camper that we actually *touched* each other.

I suppose that adolescent sexual confusion—a gift from the greatest generation, the boys who beat the Nazis and grew up listening to radio drama—has a way of knackering into sexual certainty when guys are trying to get some sleep inside pickup trucks. And as Cade Hernandez and I lay there eating Oreo cookies in the quiet black nothingness of an Oklahoma midnight, our own blank-screen radio theater played out as something like this:

A Detour in the Year We Grew Up

CADE: I need to tell you, Finn—we're about twenty miles past Dunston University.

FINN: That's one second at Earth speed. No big deal, I guess.

CADE: So. I was thinking about a lot of shit today. I'm not so sure I want to visit Dunston University tomorrow, I mean, after what happened to us today. I feel like it was kind of a sign, telling us that we should take a little detour. Or a big one.

FINN: I never really cared about visiting Dunston in the first place. I just wanted to hang out with you. And I wanted to get away from my house. I wanted to see if I could get out of the book.

CADE: Do you think you did it?

FINN: Well, for a little while today I was Cade Hernandez and you were Finn Easton.

CADE: I didn't feel like eating anyone, though. But I could go for some grits.

FINN: I'm hungry too.

CADE: Well, don't fucking look at me, incomer. Have another Oreo.

FINN: What do you think, then?

CADE: Think about what? *(There is a long pause when Finn does not answer.)* I'll tell you what I think: I've been thinking about this year, and next year too—all those miles, according to you. It was a damn good year—and that's not in any fucking book that was written out ahead of time. Monica Fassbinder. Playing baseball. Fucking with the BEST Test. Hanging out with you and Julia. Puking in Blake Grunwald's bed. Being here with my best friend eating Oreos for dinner, wherever the hell we are. Free underwear and shampoo from Governor Oldfucker.

FINN: They put dead things in shampoo.

CADE: Oh, yeah, and Mr. Nossik, too.

FINN: A ticking Nazi time bomb.

CADE: Yeah.

FINN: It was a good year, Cade.

CADE: Coming up on our last year, then who knows? It's not like it's been written down for you, dude. You could give your dad a break sometimes. You're not really stuck in anything, and we could prove it by not going to Dunston tomorrow. Take a detour.

FINN: Maybe.

CADE: And tell your dad to write another book. I need to know if you ever get laid or eat someone.

FINN: No. *(Pauses)* So you think a detour to go where?

CADE: Well. I was looking at the map, and I figure we're maybe about eight or nine hours away from Chicago.

FINN: In eight or nine hours, we will be more than half a million miles away from exactly this spot, no matter which way we go. We might as well be sitting in Chicago right now.

CADE: Dude.

FINN: What?

ANDREW SMITH

CADE: Don't you want to see her?

FINN: More than anything else I can think of.

CADE: Promise not to eat me?

FINN: You're a shithead.

CADE: Let's go to Chicago tomorrow.

FINN: You're the best human on this planet, Cade.

CADE: Swear to God you won't eat me?

The End

And just before we both shut up and fell asleep, Cade reached over and poked his index finger into my sternum and said, "A centipede with ninety-six amputations."

I wasn't wearing a shirt.

:|:

THE LAZARUS DOOR

In the State of California, things got crazy that night.

A man who identified himself as "Doctor" Nathan Pauley phoned Cade Hernandez's parents in Burnt Mill Creek and told them a ridiculous story about finding their naked and unconscious son beside a rain-swollen river in northeastern Oklahoma. He explained that *Cade Hernandez*—their son, me—selflessly dove (although I actually *jumped*) into the river in order to save the life of a trapped drowning boy and his little dog.

Their son was a hero!

Mr. and Mrs. Hernandez just kept asking the same question, which was this: Was he *sure* it was Cade he found?

So Nathan Pauley, D.V.M., said that he'd seen Cade Hernandez's California driver's license, and even copied down the plates on Cade's pickup. And he also told them that later their son acted aggressively and threatened him and then drove away—naked—before he or the sheriff's office could figure out what had happened at the river. Then Nathan Pauley asked Cade's parents about their son's heterochromatic eyes and the

"Lazarus Door" scar along his spine, and where the family actually came from.

Argentina, they answered politely.

It was ridiculous.

Look: Cade's parents did not speak telephone-English-with-a-crazy-guy-in-Oklahoma very well, but they had read the Spanish-language version of my father's novel, and they had also known me for billions of miles—ever since Cade Hernandez and I became friends. So Mr. and Mrs. Hernandez knew pretty much everything there was to know about the epileptic boy. And they realized Nathan Pauley had mistaken me—Finn Easton, the human—for their son—Cade Hernandez, another human—whom the "doctor" assumed was a fallen angel–cannibal alien here to destroy mankind.

After all, who *wouldn't* think that?

Fifteen minutes, or eighteen thousand miles, later, a man named Billy Gruber from the Craig County, Oklahoma, sheriff's department phoned *my* parents—Mike and Tracy Easton—in an attempt to track down their son. Deputy Billy Gruber told them an equally ridiculous story about something I had never done, which included being found naked in the mud below a bridge on the Little Buffalo River while performing mouth-to-mouth resuscitation on an elderly man who had nearly drowned when he accidentally drove himself, his grandson, and their wire-haired terrier dog in a minivan loaded with groceries directly into the deep and muddy river.

Finn Easton was a hero too!

Billy Gruber went on to tell my parents that apparently their son—who was actually Cade Hernandez and not me—had disappeared from the accident scene that night wearing nothing but a paper jailhouse jumpsuit, and that he had either been abducted or perhaps hitched a ride with a friendly trucker, and did they have any idea where their son, *Finn Easton*, might be heading?

"Um, Dunston University?" my dad said.

And, by the way, Deputy Billy Gruber added, had my parents ever read a book called *The Lazarus Door*? Because there was something awfully unsettling about another boy who'd been pulled naked from the Little Buffalo River too, and their son, Finn—who was actually Cade Hernandez and not me—might be in danger of being eaten.

My mother and father kept asking Deputy Billy Gruber the same question, which also was this: Was he *sure* it was their son he was talking about?

And six thousand miles, or five minutes, later, looking like confused and frightened ghosts from the flood, Mr. and Mrs. Hernandez showed up at the front door of my parents' home in San Francisquito Canyon, the site of the worst accident in the history of self-taught civil engineering.

It was a ridiculous night.

"Um, hello? Dad?"

"Finn? Where the hell are you? What's going on? Do you realize the shit we've been going through all night? Are you okay?"

"Um."

Five questions.

I had no idea where the jumping-in point to the story of the past one-point-seven million miles would be, but as I stood there in my shorts and T-shirt, outside on a street in the early afternoon with my face pressed up against a smudged black handset connected to a telephone we actually had to put coins in to operate, which, I thought, most likely contained a knackering universe of pathogens unto itself, I finally realized something.

What I realized was this: I was in my own story now, and I had the power to tell it—or not tell it—to my father.

"Normal," I said. "I am in a city called Normal, which is in the middle of Illinois, Dad."

Who'd have ever thought I'd have to go to Illinois to be in Normal?

"What are you doing there?"

"Um, I am talking on a phone that you have to put quarters in to make it work, like one of those vibrating helicopter rides for toddlers in front of supermarkets. And then Cade and I are going to drive up to see Julia Bishop, Dad."

I heard my dad sigh. Through the earpiece it sounded like fine-grain sandpaper brushing on whitewood.

"Are you both okay?"

"Yes. We're fine."

:|:

I continued. "We saw an accident where a van drove into a river. Cade and I pulled the people out of the water. That's what happened yesterday, and now we're here, in Normal."

Dad said, "Cade's parents got a crazy phone call from some doctor in Oklahoma."

"Nathan Pauley. He's a dog doctor."

"And a sheriff's deputy called us last night. We couldn't figure out who anyone was talking about."

"They thought I was Cade and Cade was me," I said. "Dad? They actually thought we were really from the book."

"I know."

"People are stupid."

Then my dad said, "I'm sorry for all this shit, Finn. It's all been my fault. Maybe I should write all those assholes another book."

"Just keep me out of it," I said. "But Cade said you could put him in it, and you could even kill him if you want."

Dad laughed. "Cade Hernandez did *not* actually read the book."

"Yes," I said. "He did. The ending pissed him off."

I had never felt so free of my father's book in my entire life. And that was precisely when I totally figured out how I—Finn Easton—could never have been trapped in my dad's novel in the first place.

Twenty miles.

Twenty miles.

"But you're okay?"

"Back to normal," I joked.

"I'm catching a flight to Chicago."

"Dad?"

"What, son?"

"Please let me do this alone. I promise we'll come home. I just need to tell Julia how the play ends."

The sandpaper sigh came again. I told my dad I loved him and hung up the phone.

• • •

I was so anxious at the thought of seeing Julia Bishop again. Although it had only been about five days—nine million miles—since we said good-bye to each other at her aunt and uncle's house in San Francisquito Canyon, it felt as though the distance had expanded infinite, endless, and I wondered how she would react when she saw me there, awkward and messy, standing nervously at her front door.

What if she didn't even know who I was anymore?

I knew it was a ridiculous thought, but millions of miles are sometimes difficult to bridge. After all, distance is always going to be more important than time.

And before we left the city of Normal, Illinois, to head north on the last leg of our trip that veered away from Dunston University and our planned-out futures, Cade Hernandez, being the natural showman that he was, decided to pick up a few items in order to construct what he decided would be the most fitting way for Finn Easton to appear at Julia Bishop's doorstep.

He told me I'd find out later.

And I said, "Just so long as it is not naked and with wings, one atom at a time."

Cade said, "Holy shit, that's exactly what I was planning."

"I feel like I should have taken a bath or something," I said. "What if I stink?"

"Dude. After yesterday, I don't care if I never get wet again," Cade said.

"Do I look okay?"

Cade Hernandez steered with one knee. He spit into his portable plastic spittoon and looked across at me.

"If I was a girl, I'd probably make out with you," he said.

"Um."

I tried to fix my unruly hair by licking my palm and brushing it. It didn't work so well.

Julia Bishop lived in a gabled two-story redbrick house with a steep slate roof and wide masonry chimneys. It sat on a street of massive homes and towering trees in a place called Lake Forest. It was not too difficult for me and Cade to find; I'd written Julia's address on the inside flap of the notebook I packed for our university visit that turned out to be not much of a university visit.

Look: It wasn't the detour Cade and I took that brought me to realize how I'd never been trapped inside my father's book in the first place. It was this: In the novel, the incomers were completely loveless. It was something that had never actually dawned on me until I stood there beside a public library in Normal, Illinois, speaking on a pay telephone with my father, whom I love, while on my way to see Julia Bishop, who loved me.

"I know now that I actually came from Earth, the planet of humans and dogs," I announced to Cade Hernandez as we drove through the streets of Lake Forest.

"Why? Because you don't want to eat me?"

"I've had plenty of opportunities to do it if I ever was hungry enough," I explained.

Cade spit.

And I said, "My dad told me he was going to write another book."

"Tell him to hurry up."

"I said he could put *you* in it this time."

270   ANDREW SMITH

"As long as I get laid and not eaten," Cade said, "which kind of gives me a boner and also makes me hungry."

Cade Hernandez's grand entrance for me was this: He'd taken panels of cardboard from a dumpster behind an electronics store in Normal and, using a black marking pen, he created a very childish-looking book prop. Across the top of the book's flap he wrote THE LAZARUS DOOR, BY FINN'S DAD. He cut a door in the cardboard rectangle so the book could actually swing open, and in the center of it, Cade drew this:

$$:|:$$

Unfortunately, the book was only about three feet tall, so the epileptic kid would have to curl up behind it to await his entrance cue. It made me feel like Laika inside her *Sputnik 2*.

We parked on the street beside the circular brick driveway in front of the Bishops' house, and Cade carried his puppet book up into the lawn where it would not be seen from the doorway.

"Now hide behind this and don't come out until I give you the signal," Cade said.

"What's the signal?" I asked.

"I don't know, but you'll know it when I give it, so don't be a dumbass. I'm doing this for you and Julia. Which reminds me, maybe I should give you those condoms."

"From your wallet? No, thanks."

"You're stupid. Now be quiet and let me go to work."

Cade Hernandez knocked on the front door. For good measure, he rang the doorbell, too. It was all very loud for a Sunday evening in a place like Lake Forest.

It was also probably not the best idea for Cade to simply

show up knocking at Julia's front door, because I could detect the suspicion in Mrs. Bishop's voice as soon as she saw him standing there. After all, neither one of us was dressed for an appearance in Lake Forest, after what we'd been through the day before and then spending the night inside Cade's sweatbox of a camper shell.

And hiding behind the facade of my father's book, this is what I heard:

The Aliens Have Landed in Lake Forest

CADE: Hi. I'm looking for Julia Bishop.

MRS. BISHOP: What do you want with Julia?

CADE: Are you Mrs. Bishop? Mrs. Bishop, my name is Cade Hernandez. Maybe Julia has told you about me?

MRS. BISHOP: Um, I don't think she has. What's this all about?

CADE: I'm a friend of hers. From California. Is she here? *(Sound of a door slamming shut)*

"Idiot!" I said from inside the book. "She's probably going to call the cops."

"Shut up!" Cade said, "That was *not* my signal."

Then I heard something at the door, and Julia's voice filled with wonder and awe.

"What are you doing here?"

And Cade Hernandez, in perfect form, said this: "I was

ANDREW SMITH

driving by and needed to poo, so I was wondering if I could use your toilet."

Julia laughed.

I assumed "needed to poo" was not Cade's signal.

"Actually, I brought something for you. A present. It's in your front yard."

Obviously, Julia's mother was standing at the door as well, because Julia said, "It's okay, Mom. This is my friend Cade, from California."

And Cade said, "Behold! It's the book!"

Julia said, "Oh."

I didn't move.

Cade repeated himself. "Ahem! Behold! It's the book!"

So I pushed the cardboard flap forward and, right there on the green lawn of Julia Bishop's home in Lake Forest, Illinois, I stepped out of the book and into Julia's arms.

:|:

I am okay.

It is the fall of our senior year. The Leonid meteor shower is coming soon, as the knackery renders comet Tempel-Tuttle into something else, and something else again.

Atoms will be scattered, and the knackery never shuts down.

During the first week of school, our campus once again was decorated with California flags and banners welcoming Governor Altvatter.

"I could use some new underwear," Cade said.

"Me too."

At first we thought that perhaps the Burnt Mill Creek High School Pioneers had once again aced the BEST Test, but that was not the reason for the governor's visit.

In fact, our school did so poorly on the BEST Test that Mr. Baumgartner—our principal—nearly lost his job for making us so dumb. At least since the unfortunate death of Mr. Nossik the school had given up on the recurring quit missions. Cade suggested they start a Quit Giving Our Teachers Aneurysms, Cade Hernandez, mission.

Like that was going to happen.

The actual reason for Governor Altvatter's visit to Burnt Mill Creek High School was to present Cade Hernandez and me with official commendations for being such heroes and saving two people's (and one dog's) lives in Oklahoma.

"You don't often find young people as brave as you two boys," Governor Altvatter said once everyone quieted down after the German slap dancers ended their ridiculous performance.

Cade nodded, looked at his certificate suspiciously, and said, "Governor Altvatter, I wear size medium in underwear."

In about thirty-six million-miles, three weeks after the Leonids, Julia Bishop is coming to visit for her Thanksgiving break from school. Since Cade Hernandez and I took our detour from Oklahoma and ended up in Julia's front yard, we have seen each other three more times.

I suppose that makes things fairly serious, although I still see myself as being too young and stupid to have sex with anyone.

Cade Hernandez agrees with the stupid part.

Laika has not reformed from the corpse-addicted dog she has always been.

And my father is writing another book.

Julia's parents overcame their uneasiness with the two sloppy-looking kids from California. They invited Cade and me in to have supper and spend the night in one of their guest rooms. Fortunately, the room had two beds, so there was no need to build the Berlin Wall again. At first, Cade Hernandez tried to goad me into sneaking out and finding Julia's bedroom, but I was so tired, I only had to listen to his words of encouragement about three times before I evaporated into sleep.

And before I did, I said, "It's been a good trip. Thank you for bringing me here, Cade."

That night, I dreamed of falling horses and bullfights and floods and a girl whose atoms must have been issued from the same calamities as mine, who appeared out of nowhere one sweltering morning and arrived in front of me at Burnt Mill Creek.

We left the following day, after breakfast. The good-bye I said to Julia was not nearly as devastating as the first time I'd said it, because I knew the miles between us had been rendered inconsequential. And I promised her that if she ever needed her boyfriend from California to come to Chicago and kick someone's ass, I could be there faster than the earth moved.

And Cade said that I was so romantic, it gave him a boner.

I fell asleep as Cade drove through Missouri.

As long as he had enough chewing tobacco, Cade Hernandez was tireless behind the wheel.

I don't know how long I slept, but I startled awake in the darkness when Cade slammed on his brakes and said, "Look at that fucking thing!"

Because this is what we saw: In the dark, walking along the gravel shoulder of a highway somewhere outside a place called Rolla, Missouri, was a man wearing a robe that glinted and shimmered in all the reflected light cast down onto the road bed by stars and moon, the knackery of the universe.

ANDREW SMITH

A set of enormous silvery wings arched up from his shoulders. He carried a sign:

I AM THE VOICE OF GOD.

The thing turned and looked directly at us as we sat inside Cade Hernandez's truck.

Cade said, "Uh."

"You don't by any chance hear anything? You know? In here?" I said. I drew a little circle in the air around the side of my head.

Cade Hernandez shook his head. "I don't think we should offer him a ride."

"Probably not a good idea," I agreed.

He gunned the engine, and we sped past the thing into the night.

:|:

A Reading Group Guide to
100 Sideways Miles
by Andrew Smith

About the Book

After losing his mother at a young age in a bizarre accident that left him with a broken back and epilepsy, Finn has been coping but never quite feeling up to meeting life's challenges. With the help of his charismatic best friend, Cade, a heroic rescue in which the two boys ultimately rescue themselves, and the risk of romance with Julia, Finn begins to see everything differently.

Prereading Discussion

Read Maya Angelou's poem "Caged Bird." Pay particular attention to images of clipped wings and shadow. Why does the caged bird sing?

Discussion Questions

1. Finn thinks about time in terms of space. He wonders about cosmological concepts and principles that hold the universe together. What does Finn's fascination with the cosmos reveal about him?

2. What does it mean to be trapped in a book? Have you ever felt trapped? How so?

3. Finn comments, "When you think about it, the universe is nothing but this vast knackery of churning black holes and exploding stars, constantly freeing atoms that collect together and become something else, and something else again." What does Finn mean by this?

4. Do you have cosmic concerns similar to Finn's? How are your concerns similar to or different from Finn's?

5. What qualities does Finn have that have allowed him to endure and eventually thrive despite the tragic and difficult circumstances of his life?

6. Finn and Cade are unlikely friends. What is the basis for their friendship? What do their differences reveal about each other? Have you ever had a best friend who was unlike you?

7. What do you think compels Cade to be provocative? What does this tell you about him? Have you ever had or wanted to have a friend like Cade?

8. What does Finn mean when he says, "I generally considered how nice it would be if I could simply stop myself from hurtling through space so fast, if only for a few seconds at a time"? Why was this stopping of movement important to Finn?

9. How is Julia's character defined by the author's portrayal of her during Finn's seizure in his living room? What was significant about Finn's response to her?

10. What drew Finn and Julia together? What does Finn admire most about Julia? What does she admire most about Finn? Discuss how their relationship changes throughout the story.

11. Finn tells the reader, "There was almost nothing about me that wasn't in his book, that didn't trap me into being something invented by someone else." Why does Finn refer to himself as *something* rather than *someone*?

12. Compare Finn's experiences during a blankout with his usual thought processes. Why is this significant in Finn's understanding of reality in the cosmos? How does Finn respond to his blankouts immediately after they occur? What does this tell you about him?

13. Do you think Finn's assessments of himself are accurate? To what extent do labels define you? Discuss ways in which you label yourself and ways in which you and your friends label each other. What are the results of doing this?

14. Images of debris, death, collapse, and abandonment are scattered throughout the novel. Explain the author's use of these images. How do they relate to the concept of the "knackery"?

15. Finn says, "I suppose love, which makes atoms sticky, is also in many ways a prison." What does Finn mean by this? How does this relate to the author's use of other images of imprisonment and the desire for release or escape?

16. What is Finn's reaction to Julia's shadow play? In what ways does Julia's shadow play help Finn better understand himself? How does it help Finn better understand Julia?

17. Why did Julia "continue to insist she did not know how her shadow story might end"? Why did this frustrate Finn?

18. Describe the reactions of Cade and Finn during the accident scene. Did Cade and Finn switch roles? How did Finn ultimately grow from this experience? How did Cade?

19. Neither Finn nor Cade stayed at the bridge to receive recognition. What does this reveal about them? How would you have reacted if you witnessed a similar accident? Would you have stayed to receive recognition?

20. Describe Finn's relationship with his father after the accident. Does he resolve his issues with his father? How does their relationship change?

21. In what ways does Finn find his true identity, rather than some shadow of a pre-scripted character?

Questions for Further Discussion

1. Why do you think Finn's father chose to name his son after the title character in Mark Twain's great American classic novel about a boy who leaves home to find himself? Have you ever had to leave to find yourself?

2. Throughout the narrative Finn refers to his best friends using their first and last names. What significance might this have?

3. Lift the book's top cover. What does the photo underneath suggest?

4. What makes Cade eventually decide to read *The Lazarus Door*? What is his response to the book? What is Finn's response to learning Cade has read the book?

5. When Finn, Cade, and Julia are together, Julia is often in the background taking photographs of Finn and Cade. Why do you suppose the author portrays Julia in this way?

6. How does learning about Julia's reason for moving from Chicago impact Finn? How does it impact their relationship?

7. How does the author present the diversity of cultural and racial differences in the novel?

8. What is Laika's mission in this story?

9. There are several commonly occurring numbers in Finn's life. How and when do they show up? What is their significance?

10. What's the significance of Finn's neighbor, Manuel Castellan, being a former bullfighter? What does Finn's bullfighter name mean?

11. How are the boy and the dog that Finn rescues from the flooding river important to the story?

Guide written in 2015 by Judith Clifton, Educational Consultant, Chatham, Massachusetts.

This guide has been provided by Simon & Schuster for classroom, library, and reading group use. It may be reproduced in its entirety or excerpted for these purposes.

Get a glimpse of Ryan Dean's senior year in this sneak peek of *Stand-Off*, the sequel to *Winger*.

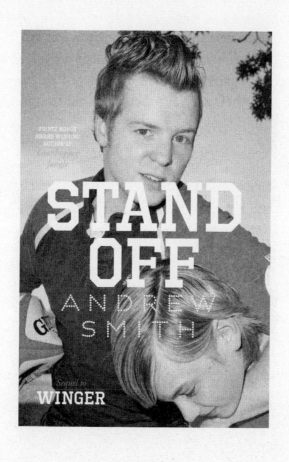

OKAY. YOU KNOW HOW WHEN YOU'RE a senior in high school, and you officially know absolutely everything about everything and no one can tell you different, but on the other hand, at the same time, you're dumber than a poorly translated instruction manual for a spoon?

Yeah. That was pretty much me, all at the same time, the only fifteen-year-old boy to ever be in twelfth grade at Pine Mountain Academy.

When you're a senior, you're supposed to walk around with your chest out and your shoulders back because it's like you own the place, right? I didn't feel that way. In fact, from the first day I got back to Pine Mountain, I was quietly considering flunking out of all my classes so I wouldn't have to move on with my life and be a sixteen-year-old grown-up.

What a bunch of bullshit that would undoubtedly be.

And, speaking of bullshit, the day I came back to Pine Mountain Academy to check in and register, I learned that I would be rooming—in a double-single room no less—with some random kid I didn't even know. It had somehow failed to sink in to my soiled-napkin brain that my last year's roommates, Chas Becker and Kevin Cantrell, had graduated from Pine Mountain and moved on to the fertile breeding grounds of adulthood, leaving me roommateless, condemned to a single-size room with two beds in it, and matched up with Joe Randomkid, whom I'd already pictured as some bloated, tobacco-chewing, overalls-wearing midwesterner who was missing half a finger from a lawn-mowing or wheat-threshing accident and owned a vast collection of '70s porn mags (since we weren't allowed to access the Internet at PM and look at real porn like most teenagers do).

Not that I look at porn, like most *normal* teenagers. I'm not like that.

But nine-and-a-half-fingered Joe Randomkid would be exactly like that, I decided.

So by the time I turned the key on my all-new, 130-square-foot boys' dorm prison cell with two twin beds, two coffin-size closets, and matching elementary-school-kid-style desks with identical 40-watt desk lamps, I already deeply hated Joe Randomkid and, at the same time, had no idea in the world who he was.

Even before I fully opened the door on our bottom-floor-which-is-usually-only-reserved-for-freshmen dorm room, I had pretty much everything about Joe Randomkid all figured out.

Joe Randomkid Ruins Twelfth Grade: A Play by Ryan Dean West

SCENE: *A very small ground-floor room in the boys' dorm at Pine Mountain Academy, a prestigious prep school for future deviants and white-collar criminals, located in the Cascades of Oregon.* JOE RAN-DOMKID, *a chubby and pale redhead from Nebraska with a stalk of straw pinched between his lips, is lying with his hands behind his head, dressed in overalls (with no shirt underneath the bib) and work boots, on one of the two prison-size twin beds, as* RYAN DEAN WEST, *a skinny, Bostonian, rugby-playing fifteen-year-old upperclassman, enters the room from the outer hallway.*

JOE RANDOMKID: Howdy! The name's Joe. Joe Randomkid. I'm from Nebraska, and my pa's a hog farmer. We have, I reckon, close to twenty-two-hundred hogs on the farm, give or take a few depending on how hungry me and my brothers are. I have ten brothers! And no sisters! Can you imagine that? Ten of them! Their names are Billy, Wayne, Charlie, Alvin, Edmund, Donny, Timothy, Michael, Eugene, and Barry, and then there's me, Joe. How come I ain't ever seen you around? Are you a new kid? I been here every year since ninth grade, but you look like you're just a kid who can't possibly be old enough to be in twelfth grade. What sport do you play? Me? I'm on the bowling team. Got a two-oh-four average, which is number one in the state in Nebraska and Oregon for twelfth-grade boys. I bet being all skinny like that, you're on swim team or maybe gymnastics. Or do you cheer? Are you one of those *boy cheerleaders*? I don't think there's nothing wrong with that at all. Cheerleading's probably more of a sport than NASCAR is anyhow. Who's your favorite driver, by the way?

Are you one of them ones who get to pick up the girls and spin them around over your head like that? If I ever did that, I couldn't help but look up their skirts, am I right? Or do you not like girls and stuff? 'Cause if you don't, that's okay too. I realize it takes all kinds. All kinds. And maybe you're from California, after all.

RYAN DEAN WEST: (*Ryan Dean West walks across the room and looks out the window.*) Now I know why they put me on the ground floor.

The End

Mom and Dad had helped me move in this time. It was weird. All the other times they'd dropped me off at Pine Mountain, it was like they couldn't possibly leave fast enough.

Dad carried in my two plastic totes. One of them contained all my clothes and boy stuff—you know, deodorant and the razor Dad sent me last fall that was still as unnecessary as ever—and the other had school supplies, some brand new bedsheets, and a microwave oven, which I had no idea why they'd insisted I bring along. I lugged in the big canvas duffel bag filled with all my rugby gear that was soon to be packed away in my locker over at the sports complex.

I wanted to play rugby again almost as much as I wanted to see Annie, whom I hadn't seen since she left Boston for Seattle five days before.

And—*ugh!*—Mom cried when she put my new sheets on the exceedingly gross, slept-on-countless-times-before, yellowing boys' dorm twin-size fucking mattress, and I just stood there, helplessly giving my dad a *what-the-fuck* look. He shrugged.

At home in Boston, I had a big bed. I'm not sure where my Boston bed fit in on the hierarchy of royalty—you know, queens and kings and such—but it was easily twice as big as a twin, if this thing even *was* an actual twin. It was probably a preemie or something—the afterbirth of a twin. So we'd had to stop at a department store in this little town called Bannock, which is about twenty minutes from Pine Mountain, to get some sheets, and the only ones they had that would fit my dorm bed following the incoming rush of PM brats were pink flannel and decorated with a winged unicorn who, according to the inscription beneath her glinting hooves, was named *Princess Snugglewarm*.

Yeah. It was going to be a great year, wasn't it?

"Why are you crying, Mom? Don't worry about the unicorns. We can hide them beneath the blanket. I checked. It only has Princess Snugglewarm on one side, so we can flip it over so it only looks a little gay," I said.

Mom sniffled. "Oh, Ryan Dean. It's not that, baby. There's only so many more times left in our lives when I'll be able to put sheets on your bed and tuck you in."

This coming from the woman who wept when she bought me a box of condoms because she actually thought Annie and I were having sex—like that was ever going to happen—when I was fourteen.

It was hopeless.

And not only do horses with big fucking spikes coming out of their heads scare me, but I hate flannel sheets besides.

ANDREW SMITH
WINGER

Ryan
Dean
grapples
with
life,
love,
and
rugby.

★ "[A] brutally honest coming-of-age novel. . . . Like puberty itself, this tale is alternately hilarious and painful, awkward and enlightening."
—*Publishers Weekly*, starred review

"Reading *Winger* is like running down a steep hill—you should probably slow down, but it feels too good to stop. A wildly original, hilarious, and heartbreaking ode to teenage confusion and frustration."
—John Corey Whaley, author of the Printz Award– and Morris Award–winning *Where Things Come Back*